Carl Weber's Kingpins:

St. Louis

Carl Weber's Kingpins:

St. Louis

Keisha Ervin

www.urbanbooks.net

Urban Books, LLC
300 Farmingdale Road, NY-Route 109
Farmingdale, NY 11735

Carl Weber's Kingpins: St. Louis
Copyright © 2016 Keisha Ervin

ISBN 13: 978-1-60162-926-5
ISBN 10: 1-60162-926-5

First Mass Market Printing July 2019
First Trade Paperback Printing October 2016
Printed in the United States of America

10 9 8 7 6 5 4 3 2 1

*This is a work of fiction. Any references or similar-
ities to actual events, real people, living or dead,
or to real locales are intended to give the novel a
sense of reality. Any similarity in other names,
characters, places, and incidents is entirely coin-
cidental.*

Distributed by Kensington Publishing Corp.
Submit Orders to:
Customer Service
400 Hahn Road
Westminster, MD 21157-4627
Phone: 1-800-733-3000
Fax: 1-800-659-2436

Chapter 1

"I don't do well with liars." A chilling voice inaded the air. "You lied to me, Donovan."

King David Mason sat behind a marble desk tapping his fingers together. Behind him on either side stood two big and bulky henchmen who were ready to pounce if given the word. Both were of African descent and wore black suits, with dark sunglasses sitting on their noses. On the opposite side of the desk sat Donovan Chambers, the man who was supposed to be in charge of all of David's finances. He was a man whom David had once trusted with his life, but upon hearing the news that he was being robbed blind David knew he couldn't have been more wrong.

"I . . . I don't know what you are talking about, King," Donovan stuttered, calling him what the streets had dubbed him. "I have done everything that you have asked of me since day one."

Donovan felt his palms and armpits begin to sweat and he wished he hadn't decided to wear the Ralph Lauren light blue button-up shirt that he had on. He blinked and hoped that the glasses on his nostrils wouldn't slide because of the perspiration starting to form on his chocolate face. He licked his thin, dry lips and blinked his brown eyes before he cleared his throat.

"Yes," King David agreed while nodding his head. "You have indeed done everything that I asked you to. You have kept my finances in order for years and kept record of every expense."

Across the desk Donovan's eyes darted from King David to the two men behind him, and back to King David. He tried to swallow, but his mouth was so dry the only thing that went down was air. "Then what have I lied about, sir?"

King David smirked at Donovan's ignorance. He was positive that Donovan knew exactly why he was in the position he was in that second. Donovan was just trying to ride the wave just in case King David really did not know about his wrongdoings. The last thing any crook did was confess to his crimes before being proven guilty. Instead of answering his questions David opened one of the drawers of his desk and pulled from it a thick manila folder. When he tossed it forward it landed with a soft thud in front of Donovan, who reluctantly opened it.

"Wh . . . what is this?"

"You can't read?"

"Yes, I can, King. I can see that these are the records of yours that I have kept up with for the past five years."

"Do you see anything wrong?"

"Not that I can tell, no," Donovan said. "I have precisely documented everything correctly. Nothing is out of place."

King David tried to give Donovan one last chance to come clean, but he saw then that he was just going to stick to his story. If he had at least been honest King David would have honored him with a quick death; now, he was going to make him suffer.

"It saddens me that I ever trusted you. Do I not pay you well? Clearly not, since over the past five years you have managed to rob me of half a million dollars. You have been shaving a little extra off the top since the beginning and I would have never known had it not been for my son, David Jr., going over all of your records. Imagine my surprise when I was informed that so much money was unaccounted for."

Donovan's eyes were wide and his lips were moving as if trying to find the words to say. His breathing became rigid and when he saw King David make a motion with his hand to the men behind him he already knew what was about to happen. He jumped up from the chair and tried to run to the exit a little ways behind him. When he reached the tall wooden door he tried the doorknob but it was useless. The door was locked from the outside.

"No! King, I can explain. I was going to pay it all back. Please don't do this to me. My wife . . . my wife she needs me, she doesn't work. My daughter is in college. She won't be able to afford her courses or her medicine. They won't make it without me. Please!"

"You should have thought about them when you made the decision to rob the hand that fed you." King David stood up and walked toward Donovan. His tall six foot four muscular frame was menacing. He fixed the collar on his suit and glared into Donovan's eyes when he was inches away from him.

"I should have replaced you a long time ago. Now you will see firsthand what happens to those who cross me. I have no remorse for you or your family, just for the money of mine that you have spent," King David said.

His henchman had made their way to Donovan and each gripped one of his arms. King David looked at them and nodded at his head of security, Mac. "Take him to the house in the woods. Make him scream. There is duct tape and a potato sack in the bottom drawer of my desk. I'll have the van brought around to the front."

With that he reached in his pocket for his keys and unlocked the door. He knew Mac would handle business accordingly. He was his oldest friend and somebody he would trust with his own life.

"No! Noooo! Nooooooo!" Donovan screamed hoping somebody would hear him.

"Remember, my office is at the top of the building. No one can hear you." King David winked at his old friend before making his exit. "Have a good night, Donovan."

He shut the door behind him and walked toward the elevator at the end of the long hallway. Before he reached it he felt the cell phone in the pocket of his suit vibrating and before he even looked he knew who it was. "Hello, honey," he said into the receiver.

"Don't 'hello, honey' me! It's almost nine o'clock and the kids are already here for dinner. Where the hell are you, David?"

"I'm leaving the office as we speak," he responded, not wanting to argue. "I stayed a little later tonight."

"I thought that bosses didn't have to work later than their employees." Her icy tone almost cut through his thick outer core, but he didn't let it.

King David sighed and stepped onto the elevator as soon as the doors opened. "I will be there," he said and disconnected the call. He knew he would have to pay for that later but at that point in time he would have done anything to avoid another argument.

"Where is Daddy?"

Angela was too busy staring at the phone not believing that David had really just hung up on her to really hear what her daughter had just said. "What, Day?" she asked.

"Was that Daddy on the phone? Where he at?"

"Umm . . ." Angela cleared her throat before turning to face her daughter, who had snuck up behind her. She got her wits together and offered a fake smile. "Your father just had a late night at the office but he'll be here in a little bit."

Davita eyed her mother suspiciously but didn't press the subject. She knew that her parents had disagreements sometimes, but somehow they always weathered the storm. So she stayed out of it. Davita was a daddy's girl definitely and people often referred to her as his shadow. Most would think it was strange that she looked up to her father instead of her mother but she didn't care; she wanted to be just like him. The only thing she didn't agree with was her name. She hated the name Davita so she made everyone call her Day. She was a beautiful twenty-two-year-old woman with smooth golden brown skin. She had high cheekbones, full lips, and round brown eyes that pierced into whatever she gazed at. On the top of her head her long, curly hair sat in a messy bun, but she made sure her edges were slicked to perfection.

"Uh-huh." She sucked her perfect white teeth and put her hand on her stomach. "Well, Ma, can I have *somethin'* to eat? You had me come over here forever ago and I haven't eaten a thing!"

She was upset because all of the food was already in place on the table in her parents' dining room; however, her mother wouldn't let her touch it. She never did until her dad got home and Day understood that, but if her mother couldn't do anything else she knew how to throw down in the kitchen. The aroma floating around the kitchen smelled amazing and it was making her even more hungry.

Angela rolled her eyes at her daughter and walked across the large kitchen to the stainless steel refrigerator so that she could grab an orange out of it. "Here, girl," she said to Day and tossed the fruit in her daughter's direction.

"Interception!"

Out of nowhere Day's twin brother, David Jr., jumped in between her and the flying fruit.

"David Jr.!" Day exclaimed, grabbing her brother's shoulder and trying to force him to give her the fruit. "Stop playin' so damn much!"

David Jr. laughed and held the orange over his head knowing that his height would prevent her from getting to it. "Say I'm the king," David Jr. taunted, grinning.

"You are out your damn mind," Day said, giving up. "I'ma just go get another orange!"

"Nope," David Jr. said, blocking his sister's way so that she couldn't pass.

"Move!" Day shouted but by then she was already laughing. Her brother really wouldn't let her through no matter which way she tried to go. "You are so annoying, David Jr.!"

The two of them were fraternal twins. David Jr. was born at 11:55 p.m. on July twenty-second and Day was born on July twenty-third at 12:05 a.m. David Jr. was a Cancer while Day was a Leo and, although they were twins, the two were as different as day and night.

Finally David Jr. gave in and gave her the orange knowing that her grin could turn into a scowl in a quickness. "Here, crybaby," he teased, calling her the name she hated as a child.

He turned to his mother and the smirk that had been planted on his face faded as soon as he saw hers. Although she smiled in their direction he saw the sadness in her eyes. In an instant his jaw clenched and he gritted his teeth before finally opening his mouth to speak again. "He's going to be late again, huh?"

Before her son could get too worked up Angela wanted to try to calm him down. She walked along the kitchen's marble floor toward him. When she was directly in front of him she forced another smile and gently placed a soft hand on his handsome face.

"It's okay, baby," she said, trying to make herself believe it. "You know your father often works past dinner."

"No, Ma." He brushed her hand off of his cheek. "That's bullshit! The food has been done for hours. Where the hell is he at?"

Day sensed her brother's frustration and immediately jumped to her father's defense. "How are you going to get mad at Daddy for missing dinner, but you're driving around in the Mercedes that he bought you? If he weren't a businessman we wouldn't have shit!"

"Watch your mouth!" Angela snapped, whipping her head toward her daughter.

Day smacked her lips and looked at her mother incredulously. "What you mean, watch my mouth? He just cursed too! You're always playing favorites, Ma!"

"Both of you watch your mouths!"

"No! 'Cause y'all aren't about to sit up here and talk down on my daddy!"

"He's my dad too, and yeah, I like my Mercedes. But that doesn't make up for him missing dinner with us. Wasn't he the one who picked Friday nights for family dinners? His schedule should have been clear."

Day started to argue back but she didn't have any words to say to his statement. He was right and she was frustrated at herself because she didn't have a response. Instead she rolled her eyes and turned to storm out of the kitchen.

"Day!" Angela called out.

"Nah, fuck this," Day said, throwing a hand up as she walked away. "I just lost my appetite. Tell Daddy I will call him. I don't want to be in this house anymore."

"Day!" Angela called again, starting to go after her daughter.

"Let her go, man," David said, shaking his head where he stood. "You know how she gets when anyone says anything negative about her father, who can do no wrong in her eyes."

Angela sighed and walked to the dark marble island in the middle of the bright kitchen. She put her elbows on the marble and put her face in her hands not knowing what else to do. She never intended to play favorites but it was no secret that she and Day had never been close. She loved both of her children but David had always clung to her, and Day to her father. Things between them had gotten seemingly better when the twins turned twenty and moved out. Still sometimes they got into disagreements that left Angela feeling low. It was clear that Day's loyalty would always be to her father, no matter how wrong he was.

"Go on in there and make you a plate to go, baby," Angela said when she finally uncovered her face. "I'm about to clean up and head to bed."

David stood there for a second not sure if he should really do as she said or stay there to comfort her. He could see the pain spelled out all over her face. He started to walk toward her and she swatted him away.

"Boy, if you don't listen to me . . ." she said. "Hurry up so I can put all that shit away."

"All right, Ma." He kissed her forehead and went to do as he was told.

Angela sat in silence and listened to the clanking sounds of David helping himself to the fried chicken, black-eyed peas, and greens that she had prepared for dinner. She sighed again and shook her head. Sometimes she didn't even know why she tried to please her husband anymore. He was cheating on her, not with another woman, with his love for dirty money. There was a point in time where the two were in love and inseparable; now they just coexisted. Whenever she brought up her unhappiness to King David he would always ask her the same question:

"What more do you want?"

To which she would always answer, "You!"

There weren't enough words in the world to get him to understand what she meant. King David felt that as long as he came home every night then she had him. He didn't take into consideration that he often came home at three o'clock in the morning when she was already in bed. They didn't spend time together; and, despite the material things that he showered upon her, they would never make up for the fact that the man she fell in love with had gone missing. What was left of him was in the pictures lacing their lavish home. That night he promised that he wouldn't be a ghost again like he had been the past two Fridays. She had even made his favorite meal and worn his favorite color: red. The long red dress that she wore draped over her slender body. She wore her hair pinned up and had even thrown on a little makeup. She had really gone overboard and he wasn't even there to appreciate it. She didn't get it and, at their age, she shouldn't have had to.

"Is there some foil, Ma?" David Jr. interrupted her thoughts.

She looked up and saw him standing in front of her holding his plate, looking very much like his father. The only difference was that at his age King David dressed like a gangster right off the streets. David Jr. was much cleaner. He stood wearing a light blue Ralph Lauren button-up with a navy blue vest over it. The tan slacks and the Stacy Adams on his feet added to his very sophisticated college-boy image.

"Give me that plate." Angela stood up from the stool she'd been sitting on. She took the foil out of the drawer next to the refrigerator and neatly wrapped her son's plate. "Here."

"Thanks, Ma." David took his plate. "I'm about to go. I love you."

"Bye, baby," Angela kissed his cheek. "I love you too."

David turned to walk away but before he was completely over the threshold of the kitchen he turned back to her. "When Dad gets home tell him I said that he ain't shit for doing this again." He didn't wait for her to respond; he just kept walking.

Looking down at the large diamond on her ring finger Angela couldn't help but to agree. She sighed and instead of going to clean up the kitchen she decided to waltz upstairs to where her other cell phone was hidden. She kept it in David Jr.'s old room simply because nobody ever thought to go in there, and he certainly didn't stay the night there.

Once there she reached under the mattress and wrapped her fingers around the device and smiled when she saw that she had three missed calls and two unread text messages. While her husband was dedicating his time to his work she had begun to feel neglected. Money could only be so much company so she used it and did something else with it. She hired an escort, but not in East St. Louis. No, everyone knew who she was there. One weekend, a year prior when King David was out of town, she took the opportunity to take her own little trip.

The man's name was Aman Grayson. He was a tall dark-skinned piece of heaven with a body to die for. He rocked the "bald by choice" look and kept his face shaved clean as well. His lips were full and his smile was perfect and straight. She had seen him with an escort service on-line that was based out of Atlanta and she almost creamed in her panties. One night with him was all both of them needed to be hooked. He was only a few years younger than her but he kept her feeling younger than the both of them.

The things he did to her body made her second-guess her own marriage.

She quickly dialed his number and listened to the ring on the other end until he picked up after the third one.

"Hey, baby," his deep voice came through from the other end.

"Hey, you," she said in a low, flirtatious voice. "I'm sorry I missed your call."

"It's cool, baby. How did the dinner go?" Aman inquired.

"He didn't show, as always. So, the kids just left so now it's just me, myself, and I."

"Mmmm," he said sexily. "I wish I were there. I've never had a foursome."

Angela giggled like a schoolgirl. "I can't wait to see you again, baby," she purred.

"I don't understand why you don't just leave him and come down here with me."

The two of them had had the conversation many times and each time Angela had to tell him why she couldn't. He didn't know who her husband was and what he was capable of. The last thing she wanted David to find out was that she was having an affair. There was no place on the earth she could go that he wouldn't eventually find her. She decided to take a different course with the conversation.

"I got the earrings you sent me. The diamonds are beautiful! They go perfectly with the bracelet you got me a little while back. You are the best, daddy." She stroked his ego, knowing that he liked to be called that.

"Say it again."

"Daddy. Daddy. Daddy." She giggled again. Below her she heard a door open and shut and she whispered, "I have to go. I will call you tomorrow."

She made a kiss sound into the phone and hung up. She slid the device back into its hiding spot and stood to her feet. She hurried and exited the room, closing the door once more, and then bounded down the stairs to greet her husband.

She met him in the dining room where he was piling his plate with food. She couldn't deny the fact that he looked good standing before her in his designer suit. He was a businessman and she loved when he dressed the part. Silently she began to undress him all the way to his . . . She quickly snapped out of her momentary lustful moment.

"Where are the kids?" he asked, looking at her on the steps.

"They left because they figured you would be a no-show like always."

"That might have been the reason for David Jr., but Davita wouldn't have left unless you pissed her off," he said knowingly.

"Whatever." Angela rolled her eyes. "You got that girl spoiled."

"And you have my son brainwashed."

"What is that supposed to mean?"

"Got him in school with them white folks like he don't come from drug money."

"I just want the best for my son."

"Look around you, Angela." King David put his hands in the air. "We are rich. As fuck. What more does he need?"

"Something legitimate!"

"I have businesses that he could run."

"Ha!" Angela scoffed. "We all know what you use your businesses for: so you don't get caught up with them taxes! Don't play with me, David."

David set his plate down on the table and walked to where his wife was standing. He wrapped his arms around her waist and kissed her on her forehead. "Listen, baby, I'm sorry for missing dinner. I'll make it up to you, I promise. Let's have a redo?"

There was something about the way his Acqua di Gio cologne hit her that made her melt into his arms. "But you always say tha—"

She stumbled over her speech when his lips found their way to her neck and began to plant soft kisses there. When he started to trace his name with his tongue there she knew she was a goner. On top of the fact that Aman had just gotten her hot and bothered, she needed something to scratch her kitty.

"Let's go to the bedroom," King David whispered seductively in her ear.

"But you were about to eat dinner."

"You got something I want to taste first." He grinned devilishly down at her and picked her up so that he could take her upstairs.

Chapter 2

A few days had passed since the failed dinner at his parents' house and David Jr. needed to clear his head. He tried to escape his thoughts by going to the computer lab of the university that he attended. He was in his senior year of school, and usually focusing on his studies brought his mind off of the chaotic world around him. Growing up David Jr. was always in his father's shadow. Everyone expected him to be just like his old man because one day he would be head of the family business. There was only one problem with that: he wasn't sure if that was what he wanted for himself. He wanted a fresh start. He wanted to start something that was his and that he could build from scratch.

David Jr. truly believed that a man should have power over his own destiny, which was why he decided to go to college right after he graduated, unlike his sister. He majored in criminal justice and kept high marks in all of his courses.

If all worked out in his favor he hoped to one day own his own law firm. At first his father was angered by the decision because he expected to have David Jr., by age eighteen, working by his side. David Jr. popped in here and there but it wasn't enough to satisfy King David's selfishness. To show his disapproval he refused to pay for his son's college education in hopes that it would sway him to come join the family business 100 percent of the time. David Jr., however, proved that he didn't need his father's money by getting a full-ride scholarship.

After seeing that his son didn't need him King David still didn't understand why his son didn't want to jump on board. Yet, he looked on the brighter side of things and knew that there was a time for everything. In fact, his son's career choice could prove to be beneficial to him in the future. David Jr., on the other hand, was torn between his loyalty to his father and his loyalty to himself. He didn't fear his father but he did respect him beyond measure. He knew what kind of pull King David had in the city and exactly what happened to anyone who crossed him.

Lately though, he had been giving his own future more and more thought. He wanted more than just fast and dirty money. When his name was said aloud he didn't want people shaking in their shoes; he wanted his name to hold honor and prestige. His family didn't understand that, not even his mother. He didn't want to be in his father's shadow and there weren't enough words in the dictionary to stress that. He remembered the day he vowed to never be like his father. It was the day that he finally understood why all of St. Louis feared him. It was because King David had no soul.

"Dad, can I get some Skittles?" nine-year-old David Jr. said from the back seat of his father's black-on-black Range Rover. He sat behind the passenger seat of the vehicle, pulling at the tie of the designer suit his mother forced him to put on that morning.

All of the kids in his class were to go to work with their parents. Since their mother was a stay-at-home mom both he and Day had to tag along with their father for the day. King David had a slew of businesses but so far they had only stopped at the salon that also had a barbershop next door, and the day spa. Day had been intrigued but David was excited to get to the night club that his father owned. Many rumors of what went on there floated around through the grapevine but he wanted to see it all firsthand. He had heard about the topless women who walked around with drink platters and the ones who danced on posts. Whenever any entertainer was in St. Louis, Club Low would be their first venue choice for their after parties. In other words, Club Low was the place to be.

"Why didn't you get none when we was just at the gas station, stupid?" Day chimed up.

King David looked back at his children in the rearview mirror and shook his head. Most twins got along well and were inseparable. His twins, on the other hand, were the exact opposite. In fact, most times he was almost certain that they couldn't stand each other. They fought like an old married couple the majority of the time.

"I wish the two of you could just get along." David sighed. "But your sister is right, David Jr. You should have gotten some at the gas station. We're about to pull up to Club Low now."

Not happy, David leaned back into the leather seat and crossed his arms. He looked at his sister with a look of annoyance on his young face and she returned it by sticking her tongue out at him. He knew she felt as if she won and he wanted to sock her in the arm.

"I hate you," he whispered so their father couldn't hear him and she responded with a smug look and a shrug of her shoulders.

King David pulled his car to the front of the luxurious building so that he could have the valet park his vehicle. Club Low was his favorite piece of property particularly because he had always wanted to own a night club when he was younger. He had even designed the entire building himself. The entire exterior was made of a dark, tinted bulletproof glass and the interior had a classy old-school feel full of tall ceilings and tan, black, or white walls. In order to get inside the guests would have to walk on the red carpet and the bouncers who stood at the doors were no joke. They had metal detectors and if you were opposed to a gun and weapon check then you instantly got the boot.

During the daytime the club served as a dine-in restaurant with a popular menu. King David figured it would be the perfect way to end the day with the twins.

"Come on, Annoying One and Annoying Two," he said, stepping out of the vehicle the moment the valet appeared and opened his door.

Day giggled and hopped out of the car. David, too, got out, not able to hide his excitement.

"Daddy, do you and Mommy ever come and party here?" Day asked in awe of the vast building.

"No, sweetheart, your mother is usually too busy shopping and doesn't have much time for

anything else." He tried to hide the bitterness in his voice but David Jr. caught on to it.

"Well, when I'm a grown-up my husband better take me to places like this. I like the finer things in life!" The smug look once again returned to Day's face as she grabbed her father's hand.

"Well, hopefully your husband keeps you as far away from me as possible," David Jr. mumbled under his breath, grasping hold of his father's other hand.

Together the three walked the red carpet, and when they got to the door the bouncers nodded their heads respectfully toward the family.

"Good afternoon, King."

"Looking sharp, sir."

They held the double doors open and when the three had made it safely through they shut them and resumed their posts.

"Whoa," David Jr. said, looking around at the décor of the place. "Dad, this is all yours?"

"Yes, and one day it will be yours." King David smiled watching his kids' eyes almost pop out of their sockets as they looked around. "In this building there is a restaurant and also multiple dance floors that serve the different music tastes of the world. I want my guests to have a good time for the money they spend at the door.

I also have an office upstairs for when I have to oversee business. Go ahead, have a look around. I'll have the chef whip us up something to eat."

The twins didn't need to be told twice. They snatched their hands away quickly and happily ran off to explore the huge building.

"Look at the ceilings, David Jr.!" Day squealed, gripping the bottom of her pink poofy Dior skirt in excitement. She threw her head back and twirled around, never taking her eyes off of the tall ceiling. "It looks like a night sky!"

David Jr. looked up and was instantly impressed as well. "I wonder how the people who did that even got so high," David Jr. wondered aloud.

"A ladder, stupid," Day responded in a "duh" fashion.

"Why you gotta talk stuff all the time, Day? Dang!"

David was tired of her already so when she went into a room that looked like a dance floor he pretended to follow her. The moment she wasn't paying attention he ran back out of the room and didn't stop until he reached an elevator at the end of the hall. Curious to see where it went he pressed the UP button and waited for it to come down to the floor that he was on. He kept looking back to make sure his nosey sister *wasn't trying to follow him. When finally the doors slid open in front of him he jumped on the elevator and pressed the "close doors" button repeatedly until they did as he wanted.*

"'Hasta la vista, baby.'" David Jr. grinned to himself, happy to finally be alone.

He remembered his father saying something about his office being at the top of the building. Curiosity got the best of him and he pressed the third floor button wanting to see what the office looked like. It didn't take long to travel up and when the elevator stopped David Jr. felt a dip in his stomach and a nauseous feeling come up to his throat. He couldn't get off that elevator fast enough. It wasn't hard to find the office simply because there was only one door and it was straight ahead. Although he knew he was up there alone David Jr. still treaded lightly, checking over his shoulder every couple of steps until he reached the door.

"Please be unlocked. Please be . . . Yes!"

David Jr. twisted the doorknob and it turned easily in the grip of his hand. Pushing the door open, David. Jr. flipped the light switch on and grinned at the office. His dad's office was one of the coolest rooms he'd ever seen. It was huge, for one, and not professional at all. There was a huge desk and a big chair behind it but that wasn't what caught David Jr.'s eyes. On the wall there was a huge flat-screen television and to the far left corner there was a basketball hoop with crumpled-up paper on the floor around it on the floor.

"Cool!"

David Jr. scooped up one of the crumpled papers on the ground and pretended that somebody was guarding him. He tossed the paper back and forth between his legs, did his signature twist move, and ended with a fade away. Once the ball was released from his hands toward the hoop he already knew he was going to hit nothing but net before he even heard the small swoosh.

"And the crowd goes wild! David Mason has scored another three points!"

He put his hands up in the air as if he really had an audience, and he took a bow. As he was coming back up to a standing position he was startled by the chime of the elevator behind him. He panicked, knowing he wasn't supposed to be in his father's office. Quickly he shut the door and looked around for somewhere to hide. Seeing a closet he turned the light back off and ran and hopped inside his temporary refuge and hoped no one would open the wooden doors and see him hiding behind one of his father's designer suits. He didn't have time to shut the closet door all the way before the office door burst open. He saw his father enter the office with two men in tow behind him; and David Jr. couldn't read his father's face but he could tell the men behind him weren't very happy.

King David took a seat behind his desk and motioned for the other men to have a seat in the two chairs on the opposite side. "Now how may I assist you two today? Please make it quick, Marcus and Juan. I have other obligations at the moment." King David cut right to the chase as soon as the men took their seats.

David Jr. peeked out and saw that the men looked to be of Mexican descent. Both were clenching their jaws as if trying to think of the right thing to say before their mouths spat out something they couldn't take back.

"You have not come through on your end of the bargain," one of the men started. "We have done everything you have asked of us."

"Yeah, so where is our money, David?" the bigger of the two said, purposely not calling him King.

King David took notice and instead of letting them see him sweat he just continued to stare at them until they were done speaking. "Before *you continue speaking, Juan, I would like to ask you if you really feel that your attitudes in this manner are truly justified?"*

"You said you would pay us the money as soon as we delivered the packages to your man in New York!"

"Hmmm. I did say that, didn't I?"

Suddenly the one named Juan brought his fist down on King David's desk with such force that David Jr. jumped from where he was in the closet. He was worried about his father's safety. Anyone with eyes could see that he was outnumbered and the two men before him looked like they hurt people for fun.

"Dad," David Jr. whispered, hoping he was not about to witness his father's murder.

"You son of a bitch! Where is our money! You owe us twenty grand!" Juan jumped up and pointed his finger in King David's face. "You black motherfucker! Where"—he banged on the desk again—"is"—bang—"my"—bang—"money?"

King David sat there unmoved the whole time, looking at the bumbling fools before him. Seeing Juan's face turning red, he chuckled.

"Sit down, Juan, before your face is bloodshot. Let's talk business." He waited for Juan to reluctantly take his seat once more before continuing. Suddenly the smile was gone from his face and

his eyes turned cold. "Now I don't know what kind of business you boys are used to running, but I guess I have to set some things straight. You come in here screaming like children making demands like I'm not the man holding all the cards. Now since you didn't answer my question I will answer it. The answer is no. Your little temper tantrum isn't justified."

King David leaned forward and rubbed his hands together and paused for a moment before he continued to speak. "To my understanding you did in fact take that package to my loyal buyer in New York, but I also am under the impression that you added your own small fee on top of that. Am I correct? You charged another thirty thousand on top of the forty that my buyer is accustomed to, and to justify this you threw my name in the mix to ensure that you got your extra money."

Juan and Marcus were quiet, not knowing what to say. They didn't think that their little hustle would ever come back to King David.

"You know, you would have gotten away with it had it not been for my buyer calling me, upset because I upped my prices without any warning. Imagine my surprise, especially knowing that you two were the ones who brokered the deal. In order to keep the peace I paid them back what you took, which means you two are sitting before me in debt, what, ten thousand dollars. So where is my money?"

Juan and Marcus were so shocked that their mouths were slightly open. Juan recuperated sooner, though, and decided to take matters into his own hands.

"Fucking nigger, I'm not paying you shit! We should have killed you a long time ago!"

Juan reached for his waist, but before he could pull his weapon, King David grabbed a switchblade that was taped to the bottom of his desk, and he threw it with force and expertise. Blood gushed out of Juan's mouth and his neck where the knife had lodged itself. He fell to the ground gripping his neck, shaking violently, and choking on his own blood.

"Juan!" Marcus jumped up but he didn't have a chance. King David had already stood up and come around the desk. He landed a hard right hook to Marcus's jaw, a left to his nose, and an uppercut to his gut.

"Oomph!" was the sound Marcus made when all the wind was knocked out of him.

"You boys lost me money," King David said from behind where Marcus had crumpled to the floor. "So now you will pay for it with your lives."

He grabbed Marcus's face with both of his hands and, with one swift motion, cracked his neck with no remorse. When he stood up he looked down at his handiwork and shook his head.

"And I just got new carpets." He sighed and reached for the throwaway cell phone in the pocket of his suit. He dialed a number and put it to his ear. "Please send a cleanup crew to my office quickly. Be discreet; my children are here."

With that he hung up the phone, turned off the light to his office, and made his exit like he hadn't just committed a double homicide.

David Jr. waited almost five minutes before he so much as moved. It felt as if his heart was about to jump out of his chest; and he couldn't believe what he had just witnessed with his own two eyes. He breathed hard and tried to get himself to calm down before he stepped out of the closet. Finally he got his wits about him and got the courage to push the door open. He was glad that the lights were off because he was sure he couldn't stomach the sight of the dead men in the room with him. He hurried to the office door and yanked it open. Once he was out of there he shut the door behind him and made *a break for the elevator. He pressed the DOWN button so many times he was sure he probably broke it. When the doors opened in front of him again he tried to run into the elevator, but he crashed into somebody.*

"Dang, David Jr.! Watch where you're going!"

Day looked at David Jr. and saw the fear in his eyes. She also noticed that his hands were shaking, and she looked curiously at him. "What's wrong with you?"

"N . . . nothing. Let's go eat."

"But I wanna see Daddy's office!"

"No!" he shouted a little louder than he had intended to. "I mean, no. We need to go down-stairs."

He pushed her back into the elevator and hur-ried up and pressed the button to the first floor. He was relieved when the elevator began to move; and he stood away from Day, trying to get his thoughts to stop going so fast. He had heard the rumors of what his father did, but a part of him never believed it. He thought his father was just a man who made money from the busi-nesses that he ran. Now he was sure that every-thing he'd ever heard about his father was true. Some people called him the boogeyman. He dis-agreed with that. The boogeyman didn't have a thing on King David.

"You're acting weird," Day said, waving her hand in front of her brother's eyes.

"Just leave me alone."

They finally reached the ground floor and made their exit. They made their way to the dining area where King David sat waiting for them at a table with two empty seats.

"There you are! Where were you two?" He eyed them suspiciously when they got to the table. His eyes lingered on David Jr., who couldn't seem to look him in the eye.

Day wasn't sure what was going on, but something told her not to tell her dad that they were on the third floor. "We were on the second floor going through all the dance floors," she lied, and took her seat. "Huh, David Jr.?"

"Yeah," David said and sat down in front of his plate. "We were on the second floor."

King David eyed them more suspiciously but didn't say anything else; he just motioned to their food. "Well, dig in! Your mother will kill me if she found out I didn't feed you after a long day out!"

David Jr. remembered that as one of the toughest meals to stomach.

"Ay, foo'!"

David Jr. looked up from the computer he was sitting at and grinned when he recognized the voice that had interrupted his studies. "What's good, Ro!" He stood up to greet his best friend, Roland Gray, with a handshake.

"What's good? What's good ain't in this computer lab! Do you ever take a break?"

"I was just tryin'a clear my head, that's all," David Jr. said and then peeped that his boy was dressed like he was about to step out. "I see you got fly. What's going on tonight?"

"Shit, just a frat party up the street. You should slide through with me!"

David Jr. contemplated it for a second before smiling and nodding. "A'ight, coo'. Let me go to the crib first and get dressed."

"Nah, for real," Ro joked, peeping his boy's sweats. "'Cause I'm not rolling to where bitches is gon' be at with a dusty nigga."

"Fuck you." David Jr. laughed. "Follow me to my crib and I'll drive."

Chapter 3

Day sat before the vanity mirror in her room and smiled at her reflection. She knew she was beautiful and she didn't need anybody to remind her. The shiny mocha-colored lip gloss accented her full lips perfectly and she batted her natural, long eyelashes.

"Whenever you're done admiring yourself I got something else that would love your attention," a voice behind her said.

She averted her eyes in the mirror and looked at the half-naked man lying down on her king-sized bed. He was stroking his erect manhood and staring back at her seductively. She smirked and licked her lips at him before standing up from her stool to join him in bed. On her body she wore only a matching pink lace bra and panty set, with a cream-colored silk robe draping from her right shoulder. She got to the foot of the bed and climbed on. She sat on her knees, undid her robe, and began to tease her watcher.

"Tony, do you like it when I"—she used her perfectly manicured hands to rub her full breasts—"touch myself?"

"Yeah," Tony said and looked thirstily at her hands going down her toned stomach to her crotch. He was a muscular man with pecan brown skin, a beard that stayed perfectly trimmed, and a baby face that kept him out of trouble . . . for the most part. He was one of her father's hired hands, which was how they met.

"Do you want to hear how wet I am, baby?" Day asked and when he nodded his head yes she slid her panties to the side and exposed her fat pussy lips and her swollen clit. She began to roll the middle finger on her right hand on it in a circular motion, pleasuring herself before she slid it inside of her. "Mmmm!"

"Yeah, baby," Tony said. He was enjoying the scene before him and could not wait to dive into her gushy goodness. "Just like that. Damn, you sound so wet!"

Day fingered herself almost to the point of climax, but then she stopped. She bit her lip and looked at his penis standing at attention. "Are you ready for me?"

"Yeah."

"Mmmkay, but first you have to do something for me," Day said, sliding the robe completely off of her shoulders. "I want you to rip my bra and panties off, and fuck me like you hate me. Can you do that? I want you to make me scream, Tony."

Tony's eyes lit up at the request. Ever since he had first laid eyes on Day he knew she was a freak, but he never knew exactly how much of a freak she was until that very moment. He removed his boxers completely and sat up so that he could comply with her request. He used one of his buff arms to wrap around her slim waist while the other grabbed a handful of her natural, straightened hair. He leaned in to kiss her but she put a finger to his lips.

"Kiss me everywhere but my mouth," she said sweetly; but there was something about her tone that told Tony that she was serious.

Instead of making a big deal out of it he did as he was told and put his tongue on her neck. He licked and sucked it so good she had tingles surging through her body. Without warning he gripped her bra and ripped it from her body. The snap stung but it accented the mood and Day moaned loudly and bit her lip. Cupping her breasts Tony massaged the areolas with his thumbs before popping them in his mouth at the same time. He suckled on them like he needed milk from them, causing her to throw her head back in ecstasy. His left hand found its way to her warm pussy and he moaned softly when he felt how wet she was.

"Take these off," he grunted and ripped them off too.

"Tssss," she hissed at the sting.

"Lay your ass down," Tony said and flipped her over on her back and reached to the nightstand for a condom. He opened it and slid it on with one hand, barely giving Day a chance to catch her breath. "Fuck you like I hate you, huh?"

Day didn't have time to respond when she felt him ram his full thick eight inches deep inside of her. She was dripping so it didn't take much force to get all inside but still it came as a shock.

"Ahhh!" she cried out. "Yes! Fuck me! Fuck me!"

He pounded in and out of her love box, wetting the sheets under them. He sucked and bit on her neck while one hand pinched her nipple. He enjoyed the way she threw it back up at him, making all of his thrusts even more powerful.

"This is some good pussy!" he yelled, clenching the pillow under her head with his free hand. "Get on top."

That was exactly what she hoped that he would request. She couldn't lie; he was putting it on her so good she almost forgot why he was there in the first place. She let him switch their positions and she straddled him. She slid down on him slowly, watching his face twist in pleasure. She grabbed his hands and placed them on her plump behind, and as she rode him she made her cheeks jump one at a time. She was trying to get him to bust soon but she felt herself coming to a climax. Her clit started to tingle and she knew it was almost that time so she rode harder and faster.

"Uh! Uh! Uh! Uh!" she moaned. "I'm about to come. I'm about to cum!"

"Me too," Tony said, holding on to her waist tightly and mashing her down on his throbbing shaft. "Come with daddy, baby."

It only took two more pumps for Day to squirt all over his stomach and for him to shoot his homeless children into the condom. Day's body was shaking from the force of the orgasm and from the looks of it Tony seemed as if he was about to pass out. Not wanting to miss her opportunity Day stood up from the bed and kicked Tony's pants by the door so that he would not have easy access to them. She grabbed her robe from the bed and put it on.

"That was some good pussy, girl," Tony said, covering his face with his hands. "You have gold between those legs of yours. I have never nutted in under twenty minutes before today."

"Good," Day said and waltzed back over to the black vanity. She slid the top drawer open and grabbed the shiny 9 mm pistol from it. "Seeing as how that was the last nut you will ever bust in your life." She aimed the gun at him and laughed at his shock.

"Yo, what the fuck? Why you playin' with me, girl?" Tony's eyes widened at the sight of the gun. He looked down on the ground for his pants and his own weapon but saw that they were nowhere close. "What's going on, Day?"

"Now it's 'what's going on, Day?'" Day mocked him. "Boy, did you think I was really interested in you? You ain't shit but a flunky who works for my daddy. Word on the street, though, is that you're the one who let them cats from Staten Island in at Club Low when they started shooting."

Tony's jaw clenched and he didn't say anything. That let Day know that she was correct. She shook her head and rolled her eyes. That night cost them a lot of lives, and a couple of feds were on their necks. King David couldn't move the way that he wanted to because too many eyes were on him and it was all Tony's fault. Not only had he set that up, word on the streets was that he was working with the feds to get enough information about the illegal portion of King David's business, and that couldn't happen.

They would all go to prison for life, so Day made it her personal job to fix the problem.

"You fucking bitch," Tony spat as it dawned on him what was happening. "You set me up."

"And got some dick while doing so." Day smirked.

"You can't kill me," Tony boomed boldly and actually stood up. "As soon as you pull that trigger your crib will be swarming with feds."

"Awww," Day crooned, stepping to the side, not wanting him to get close to her. "That's cute, you think you have leverage. But let me tell you something, baby boy: you remember when we were at the restaurant? And you set the jacket to your suit behind your chair? Our waitress was a hired hand. She removed that little tracker you were wearing when she served our food. Feds-ass nigga."

Day couldn't help herself. She fired her weapon and caught him in the shoulder. Tony yelled out in pain but Day wasn't done. She ran up on him and hit him in the face with her left fist. When he stumbled she pulled the trigger again, this time catching him the gut.

"My father worked too fucking hard to get us to where we are at for a pussy-ass nigga like you to stop us!"

He fell on the ground holding tightly on to his wounds, gasping for air; but Day didn't care if none found its way to his lungs. She stomped his face with her bare foot and spat down at him.

"Die," she said coldly and emptied the clip in his face.

When she was done with him he was not recognizable. She calmly set the gun down on her vanity and made a phone call on her TracFone.

"Hey, Marlin," she said sweetly when her father's old friend answered. "Yeah, Daddy's been real good. David Jr. and I have been too. Listen, I have a little situation at my house. I need a cleaner team as soon as possible. And can you please make sure they have the color carpet I like this time? Thanks!"

"I told you all the bitches were gon' be here!"

Roland and David Jr. stood in the midst of what looked to be a wild college party going on before them. The atmosphere was exactly what David Jr. needed to take his mind off of his seemingly difficult life. As soon as he had stepped into the building he noticed that many of the "bitches," as Roland had referred to them, had eyes trained on the two of them instantly. It wasn't an uncommon thing; the two handsome young men were what most women called "pretty boys." It never failed; most of their outings together ended with at least one of them getting some play.

"Hi, David," a pretty redhead cooed, stopping in front of him.

David Jr. recognized her face as one that was in a college class of his. He couldn't deny that she was beautiful, but David Jr. was one who wasn't really down with the swirl. He loved his black sisters too much to ever even think about crossing that line. Even if it was just sex, he felt as if he was betraying the woman who birthed him. He also felt that if things ever went too far a white woman would never fully be able to understand him. Instead of indulging too much in the girl's conversation, David Jr. gave her a small smile and head nod before walking away. He felt slightly bad for embarrassing her in front of her friends but that was better than leading her on.

He and Roland made their way to the living room area of the frat house, but before David Jr. was able to get comfortable he connected eyes with someone who had no business even looking his way. Sheila Braxton was a caramel female with a big chest and an even fatter ass. She subtly licked her lips his way and he had to chuckle because he had literally seen her hanging off of her boyfriend Lucas's arm when he had first entered the party. She was watching him as an eagle would watch its prey and there was something about the way her eyes were on him that made him rise in his 501 Levi jeans.

"Ay, I'm gonna see what they're on over there," Roland told him, pointing to a table where a group of people were playing beer pong.

"All right," David Jr. said, not taking his eyes off of Sheila.

Damn, she thick, he thought when Roland left. He eyed her curiously when she began making her way over to him. Instinctively he looked around to see if Lucas was close by. The last thing he wanted to do was get into a fight with a man over his bitch when she was being thirsty.

"What's up, DJ?" she purred into his ear when she sat next to him on the couch. He could smell the liquor on her breath; however, that wasn't enough for him to avert his eyes from her.

"Who is DJ?" David Jr. asked, raising an eyebrow. "You can call me David Jr."

"Ohhh." She giggled. "Feisty! I like that. Okay, David Jr., what's up?"

"Nothing, just chilling. Where your man at?"

"Why you worried about him?"

"Because you're lookin' at me like you want this dick, and I'm not tryin'a have no problems because of a bitch."

"Bitch?" Shelia pouted, and David Jr. couldn't tell if she was playing or if she was serious.

"My bad, Sheila," he said, trying to clean up his words. "You know what I mean, though. You and Lucas are tight. What you on?"

"Well," she said, and grinned at him devilishly. "There are vacant rooms upstairs, so if you're down I'm tryin' to be on you."

David Jr. grinned at her words and licked his lips. On the lowest of keys he had been wanting to know what it felt like to dig all up in her guts for a while, but Lucas was always all up in the mix. He usually was the type to respect a relationship; but she was basically throwing herself at him, and the liquor in his system was blocking his conscience.

"What about Lucas?"

"That nigga probably somewhere around here chasing one of these white girls," she said and grabbed his hand. "Come on. Let's go upstairs."

Without thinking he stood up with her and followed her to one of the staircases that led to the upstairs part of the house. Everyone was so busy drinking and chasing women that their exit wasn't even noticed. David Jr. couldn't help it. On the way up the stairs he reached and squeezed Sheila's soft, plump apple bottom. Once they had made it up the staircase and

hit a corner he pinned her up against the wall
and put his hand under her blouse so that he
could squeeze her breasts. Using his thumb and
pointer finger he massaged one of her nipples
and ground his crotch into hers.

"Mmm," she moaned softly, feeling herself get
moist. "I heard you were a freak, too."

"Shut up," David Jr. said and lifted her shirt
up. His mouth met the nipple he was playing
with and he sucked it like he was thirsty.

He was beginning to feel the couple of shots he
had downstairs start to take effect and the only
thing he wanted to do was satisfy the bulge in
his pants. He used his other hand to go between
her legs and under her skirt. Barely surprised
that she wasn't wearing any panties, he used his
middle finger to massage her clit, causing her to
squirm uncontrollably.

"Wait," she breathed, pushing him back some.
He thought she was having second thoughts but
when she nodded toward one of the bedrooms
he knew that she was still game. "Let's go in
there. I don't want someone to see us fucking
in the hallway."

David Jr. allowed her to grab his hand and
lead the way. His eyes were trained on the way
her ass jiggled in the black body con skirt she
wore so he barely paid attention to the bedroom's surroundings.

"The closet." Sheila smiled kinkily back at him. She opened the tall white door of the walk-in closet and took a step inside. "I want you to fuck me in this closet, David."

David Jr. responded by shutting the door behind him and grabbing her up by the waist. He pushed her far back into the wall and lifted her skirt up. He couldn't get the feeling of her pussy off of his fingers and he wanted to touch it again. David could tell she was freshly shaved when he shoved his finger inside of the hole that the wetness was dripping out of. Using two fingers to sex her, he let his thumb massage her clit while he sucked her neck.

"Uh! Uh! Uh!" Sheila moaned in David Jr.'s ear, letting him know that he was hitting her spot. She lifted one of her legs up so that his hand would have better access, and she started to gyrate her hips. "You gonna make me come already, David. Your fingers feel like a dick!"

David Jr. said nothing; he just kept flicking his wrist in the dark and letting his other hand fondle her body until he felt her juices flow freely.

"Yessss!" she hissed, feeling her first nut come on. She couldn't believe he had just done that by only using his hands. Lucas had never pleased her in such a way and she wanted more. She leaned in to kiss David Jr. on the lips but he pulled his head back. Their eyes had adjusted to the dark and she could see him shaking his head.

David Jr. let her go and took a step back. The sound of a belt buckle being unfastened along with the sound of him dropping his pants could be heard.

"Get on your knees," he instructed. "Suck my dick."

Sheila excitedly did as she was told and dropped to her knees. She felt the softness of the carpet on them and she reached for David Jr.'s crotch. She moaned softly when she felt how big and hard he was and she pulled it out as fast as she could. Sheila was so good at sucking dick she could give Super Head a run for her money.

The moment he felt her mouth on it David Jr. knew that those big lips she had were good for something. She sucked and slurped like her life was depending on it and the sounds David Jr. made only made her suck harder. He grabbed the back of her weave so that he could hold her still while he pounded her face, and when he knew he couldn't take anymore he made her stand to her feet.

"Bend over," he said, bending down and grabbing a condom from the pocket of his jeans. "And don't tell me to stop."

"Mmm," Sheila said and bent over what seemed to be a tall shoe rack. She gripped on to the metal and prepared for the monster to enter her cave. "Okay, baby."

Sheila wasn't his girl, or anybody to him for that matter, so he had no intention of going easy on her poor kitty. As soon as the condom was on, David Jr. forced her back to arch and he dove right in. He pounded in and out of her wetness relentlessly, relishing the way her walls gripped his shaft.

"Fuck," he said to himself, biting his shirt. He slapped her ass and dug deeper into her love canal.

"Yes, daddy!" Shelia squealed and threw it back at him. Her eyes were clenched shut as she tried to take the D. She wanted to show him that she was a big girl, and in the back of her mind she was already preparing to give Lucas the boot. "Fuck me harder!"

The only sounds that could be heard were her moans, David Jr.'s pants, and the soft sounds of the music playing downstairs. David Jr. felt the tingle in his tip and knew he was about to let go.

"Ahhhhh!" Sheila screamed into the darkness of the closet, letting him know that she had reached her second climax.

"Shiiit!" David Jr. threw his head back and released inside of the condom.

He waited a couple of seconds to catch his breath from the strength of his orgasm before he slid out of her. He took the condom off and threw it to the side, not caring who found it later. Sliding his boxers and jeans back on he checked his pockets to make sure he still had his phone and car keys before flipping on the light switch. Sheila was fixing her blouse with a damp forehead and smitten eyes. Eyes that were on him.

"Soooo . . ."

"So what?" he said, buckling his belt.

"So you're just gon' bust your nut and bounce?"

David Jr. grinned and shook his head at her. "Somethin' like that," he said. "Your boyfriend is downstairs and he's probably looking for you." With that, he opened the door of the closet and let some fresh air into the stuffy closet.

"I'll see you around." He stepped into the bedroom and shut the door behind him before she could say another word.

He knew he was in one of the frat boy's rooms by the half-naked women on the posters draping from the wall. He had almost made it to the bedroom door when it burst open suddenly.

"Damn, nigga! I been looking for you everywhere!" Ro stumbled into the room with a bottle of Crown Royal Apple hanging loosely from his hand. "Come on, we gonna take some more shots."

David Jr. laughed at his drunk friend and shook his head. "Nah, dog, it looks like you done had enough shots!"

"Fuck you, nigga!" Roland sat on the bed.

Shelia must have thought she'd waited in the closet long enough and that when she made her exit nobody would be in the room. She was wrong and the look of surprise that read on her face when she and Roland connected eyes was priceless.

"Damnnn, nigga! You hit Sheila?"

David Jr. started laughing but Sheila's face turned beet red. She turned her nose up at Roland and rolled her eyes. "Shut the fuck up! He ain't hit shit!"

"'Why you always lyinnnn','" Roland taunted in a singsong voice.

Shelia looked like she wanted to slap him sober but instead she stomped out of the room.

"These bitches ain't shit, man," Roland shook his head. "She probably gonna go kiss on that nigga knowing damn well she was just sucking dick!"

"You're a fool!" David Jr. doubled over, laughing. "Come on, bruh, let's go back downstairs to the party. I think I saw some hot wings in the kitchen and I need parts!"

Chapter 4

The sound of the alarm clock blaring from the phone by his face jarred David Jr. out of his sleep. He moved slowly to turn it off and then wiped down on his face. He already knew what time it was: eight in the morning. Time for his criminal justice class and he seriously was debating skipping it, except he had an exam that day that he couldn't afford to miss.

"Why did I let that nigga talk me into going out last night?" He sighed to himself and sat up in his king-sized bed.

The sun was already peeking through his drapes and he knew then that the alarm had not made a mistake; it was time to get up. He swung his legs over the side of his bed and stood up. Looking down he saw he was still wearing the same boxers as he was the night before, and he turned his nose up knowing what his mother would say if she knew: "Go wash your balls, nasty!"

Tired was not the correct word to describe what he was. After he dropped Roland off at his car and finally got into his house it was almost three in the morning. He made to take a cold shower before throwing some clothes on and brushing his teeth. After grabbing a brush for his hair he snatched up his book bag and car keys so that he could make it to the café in the school cafeteria before his exam. He half walked and half jogged down the stairs of his condo, brushing his hair so that his waves were intact for the day ahead of him.

When he finally reached the school the first place he headed was toward the cafeteria so that he could get some caffeine in his system. He wasn't worried about his knowledge of what would be covered on the exam, but he was worried about his attention span. He didn't want to fall asleep halfway through the test and fail because he'd only answered half of the questions.

Although it was early the cafeteria was flooded with students trying to put something in their stomachs before their morning classes. He was just thankful that the place was seemingly quiet to have as many bodies as it did. The café's name was Java Joint and it had its own little area away from the other parts of the cafeteria. You had your choice of a booth or a tall table to sit at, but that day David Jr. would choose neither.

As soon as David Jr. took his place in line a wonderful perfume hit his nostrils. He stared at the woman in front of him and figured it was coming from her. Her long, natural, curly hair was sitting on top of her head in a messy bun. He was about to compliment her scent so that she would turn around so he could see her face, but it was her turn to order next.

"May I have a caramel mocha latte? With extra whipped cream, please."

Her voice was soft and very feminine. David Jr. liked it. The older woman ringing her up gave her a chubby when she handed her what she'd ordered.

"That will be $5.50 with the extra whipped cream, please," the woman at the register said.

When the girl reached in her over-the-shoulder Coach purse to grab the matching wallet, David Jr. stopped her.

"Don't worry about it. Ms. Lynn, can you make that two caramel mocha lattes?" Before the girl could object to him paying for her drink, David Jr. pulled out a twenty from his pocket and handed it to Ms. Lynn.

"David Jr., always the charmer, huh?" Ms. Lynn winked at him and went to go blend the second latte.

In front of him the girl whipped around and looked into his eyes. He was in awe. She was the most beautiful girl he had ever seen. She was petite, but had a nice round bottom. Her facial features looked to be crafted by Michelangelo himself. High cheekbones, slim nose, full pink lips, and cheekbones so high any model would feel threatened. It wasn't until she glared at him that he snapped out of his trance.

"I don't need you paying for my things," she said venomously.

"Whoa, whoa!" David Jr. threw his hands up. "I was just trying to be chivalrous."

"Mmm." The girl stepped back and sized him up. "Chivalrous my ass. Literally."

"What's that supposed to mean?" David Jr. looked at her with a confused expression on his face. "I was just trying to be a nice guy."

"Yeah," she huffed and grabbed her coffee. "And were you just trying to be a nice guy when you took that girl upstairs at the party last night?"

David Jr.'s jaw almost hit the tiled floor and he had nothing to say.

"Exactly," the girl said and started to switch away.

Not wanting her to leave without him at least getting to know her name, David Jr. grabbed his coffee from Ms. Lynn and hurried after her.

"Hey wait!" He grabbed her arm softly, making her stop in her tracks. "That's not what you think it was!"

"Then what was it?" She put her hand on her hip and sipped her drink.

Stuck again, David Jr. rubbed the top of his head and grinned sheepishly. "Okay, well, maybe that was what you thought it was. Wait!" He stopped her from walking away from her. "But that's not what this is. I honestly just wanted to tell you that you smell nice. Okay, wait, that sounds weird as fuck. Can we start over?" He held his hand out. "My name is David Mason Jr. Everybody calls me David Jr., though. I hate DJ."

She looked at his hand for a minute and then eyed him suspiciously. "David Mason Jr.? As in *the* David Mason's son?"

David Jr. shrugged his shoulders and for once was happy about being tied to his father. "Yeah, that's my pops."

"Hmm," the girl said, and then after a moment took his hand in hers. "My name is Indigo . . . and I'm still not interested."

She winked at him before stepping around him and walking away. Something about her had intrigued him and he couldn't quite put his finger on it. Whatever it was, he knew that this wouldn't be his last time seeing her.

"This is such a lovely restaurant." Angela beamed around at the beautiful restaurant that King David had treated her to for lunch. "I absolutely adore these ceilings!"

King David took a drink from his glass of
water and looked at his wife with wonder in his
eyes. He had paid the owner of a well-known
Italian restaurant, Atello's, so that he and his
wife could enjoy a nice quiet lunch. Staring at
her he had to admit that she was still the most
beautiful woman he had laid eyes on, on the
outside. But gone was the woman he thought
she was on the inside. She never quite could
understand why he stayed out so late, especially
if he wasn't cheating. It was simply because he
couldn't stand pretending to be happy with her.
Yes, the sex was still good and yes, she was a
good mother, for the most part.

"Why do you talk like that?"

"Like what, honey?" she asked, confused by his
question.

"Like you don't come from where I come from."

Angela had just picked up her glass of wine but
had to set it right back down on the red tablecloth.
She and her husband sat on opposite sides of a
small, circular table, so when she looked up she
was looking directly in his eyes. She thought
he was kidding for a second, but when she saw
the seriousness in his eyes she scoffed.

"David, you come from the hood. I don't. So
what is it that you are trying to say?"

King David chuckled before grabbing a Cuban
cigar from the table and lighting it. He took a

long drag from it before he responded. "You're right. You aren't from the ghetto like me, but we went to the same school. So sorry to have offended you."

Angela sighed and, instead of snapping back at him, reached across the table and grabbed his hand, slightly massaging it with her thumb. She had to remember the real reason why she had requested that they go out to dinner in the first place. She cleared her throat and forced her smart remark back into the furthest depths of her mind.

"Baby, I'm just complimenting your taste. That's all. You don't have to attack me just because I have elevated my vocabulary from when we were younger. Anyway, have you talked to those children of ours?"

Although suspicious of her sudden change in topic, especially when the Angie he knew was quick to fire off at the tongue, he let it go. "I talk to Day every day. David Jr. hasn't been answering my phone calls. But that is nothing new."

"You need to talk to him, David. He's your heir, isn't he? Maybe you should make him owner of more of a percentage in your business. Give him more responsibility and maybe he will come around the office more."

"And what about Davita? I can't up his ownership if I don't do hers."

"And why can't you?"

"Because it wouldn't be fair."

"I don't understand why you have that girl running the streets like one of your . . . goons anyway! She is a lady and she needs to be in school!"

"I hate to break it to you," King David said, and took another pull from his cigar, "but Davita is nothing like your precious David. She has the heart of a lion and better aim than most men I've come across. I'm not sure if I could say the same about David Jr."

"Maybe he wants more for himself that to tote around guns all day."

"That comes with his last name. You know what I've had to do to give you all the life that you have always wanted. Now you mean to tell me that he's too good for it? And you expect me to give him even more of my assets when he doesn't even want the ones he has? If anybody deserves more shares it is Davita."

"She isn't your heir. . . ."Angela let her voice trail off.

"And why can't she be? Because she isn't a boy? If you ask me she is leading that race, because she actually cares to learn my teachings. She understands the Mason way while David Jr., he seems to be doing everything in his power to not be like me. And it seems like you are doing everything in your power to make sure he is the twin to get all of my money."

"He deserves it!"

"How? Besides have my name what has he really done for the Mason name? I can't even tell you how many times Day has made me proud, but him? He hasn't done anything but resent me since he was a child."

Angela clenched her jaw because that was something that she couldn't argue with. She couldn't count on her hands or feet anymore how many times she had heard her son say those very words. Most men, especially those named after their fathers, yearned to be just like them. Her son, on the other hand, was doing all that he could to run the opposite way. And although she supported his decision she just couldn't let him go too far. Her and her husband's eyes stayed on one another for some time until their food finally came. Angela lifted her fork up and played with her shrimp for a moment before she reluctantly placed her fork back down.

"How did this happen?" she whispered to the tablecloth. "How did we end up here?"

He took a bite of his steak and eyed her, almost confused that she didn't know. He reflected on the first day they met.

"Give me your money, punk!" said a kid at least two sizes bigger than a sixteen-year-old

David Mason. Still, he stood in the hallway of his high school, fearless. It was his first day at his new school and he knew it was only a matter of time before somebody tried the "new kid." David was skinny for his age, and his clothes were a little ragged. His mother worked two jobs to keep a roof over his head and most times she couldn't afford to buy him new clothes to keep up with the fashions of the other kids. So he made do with what he had; material things didn't mean much to him. He was just happy to be able to come home and find food on his table.

"I don't got no money," David said and tried to walk around the kid.

"Mothafucka, I said give me your money!"

The bully pushed David back to the same spot that he was just in. He had a couple of his own friends behind him goading him on and laughing. They just knew their boy was about to lay a hurting on the new kid.

"Yeah, give him your money, little nigga! We tryin'a go to the arcade after school!"

David looked at the three people in front of him and, out of the corners of his eyes, he studied the small crowd forming around him. He could always run and get a teacher, but coming from where he came from, running away from a fight was something that you couldn't live down. Also, he could run and get help but the problem would still be there the next day, and the next day. Instead he gave the boys a fair warning.

"This ain't what you want, man," he said, putting his arms up.

Instead of heeding his warning, the big ring-leader boy laughed and threw his own hands up, mimicking David. "You must not know who I am, mothafucka! I'm Big Larry and what I say goes in this school." Big Larry walked up on David and grabbed the collar of his shirt, pulling him close so that he could talk directly in his ear. "Do you hear me? Now give me your money, bi—"

Before he was able to finish the insult David yanked away so fast that Big Larry didn't have a chance to react. David hit him with a left and right hook combo so quick and powerful that Big Larry stumbled back with his face up to the ceiling. When David saw his friends trying to jump in on the action, he pushed Larry's big body into one of them so he could handle the other, one on one. David busted his lip with a right and then landed a left to the boy's right temple, dropping him instantly. He advanced on the other boys on the ground and proceeded to stomp both of their heads into the marble floor of the school. When he was done David leaned down and grabbed the hood on the back of Big Larry's sweatshirt, lifting him up so that he could speak directly into his ear.

"You must not know who I am, mothafucka. I'm David, and if you try me again I will slit ya fuckin' throat!"

David threw his head back down, causing it to make a sickening thud, before he walked away. The crowd cleared a path for him to go through and he heard a lot of cheers.

"Damn! That boy just beat the shit out of Big Larry and his crew!"

"Mmm, that's just embarrassin'!"

"They dead?"

Before any teacher could show their face David hurried up so that he could exit the building and go home. What David had failed to mention to the boys was the reason he was a new kid. David had a thing for getting kicked out of school for fighting. People often picked on him until he was forced to lay hands on them. At his last school he beat a boy so bad he would be deaf in his left ear for life. This time, though, David hoped that nobody would run their mouths simply because he didn't want to put his mother through that again. The high school he was at was the last one in their city that would accept him, so if he got kicked out then they would have been forced to move. He knew his mother didn't have the money to do that so he was trying to be on his best behavior. Honestly, he hadn't done half of what he wanted to do to Big Larry, but he was sure the message he sent was loud and clear: don't mess with the new kid.

On his way down the stairs a book fell out of his book bag but he had no idea.

"Hey!"

He heard a voice behind him but still he did not stop to turn around and see who it was.

"Hey! Stop. You dropped this!"

Hearing that he had dropped something, he turned around and was surprised to see a pretty, brown-skinned girl wearing a white blouse and tan slacks. Her hair was pulled up in a neat ponytail and the braces on her teeth gleamed in the sun. She held the textbook out in his direction and he walked back toward the stairs to retrieve it from her.

"You definitely don't want to lose that. You won't be able to graduate if you do."

"Really?" David asked, placing it back into his bag, this time making sure it was zipped up all the way. "That's stupid."

"They spend good money on those books." She shrugged. "They want their shit back."

Not expecting a girl like her to use such foul language, the fact that she cursed caught David completely off guard. She saw his surprise and started to laugh.

"What? Girls can't curse now? We can't give you men everything!"

It was David's turn to laugh; however, he did so sheepishly. "My bad, I ain't mean to look so shocked. You just too pretty to have to use words like that."

The girl smiled at him, pleased at his compliment. "Oh, so you can fight and you're smooth with the ladies. I see. You must have the whole package."

Suddenly David was embarrassed. He didn't want a girl like her seeing him behave so savagely. Most times people saw that they just boxed him in and deemed themselves right for stereotyping him. Just a typical black hoodlum.

"So you saw that, huh?" *David looked down at his black Nike sneakers, avoiding her eyes.*

"Yes," *she said, and put her hand under his chin so that she could lift his head back up.* "It's about time somebody gave those assholes a taste of their own medicine! I don't see them messin' with nobody for a while! You just saved a lot of people today, and you don't even know it."

"Just your typical Robin Hood from the hood, huh?" *He grinned at her.* "I'm David. What's your name?"

"Angela Smalls," she responded, and put her hand out. Awkwardly he shook it and once again the two burst into a laugh.

"You look like you live on the other side of town. Let me walk you to the bus stop." He nodded his head down the stairs and toward the bus stop not too far.

Suddenly, any sign of the laughter once sprawled there was removed from Angela's face. *"Why do you assume I live in the other part of town?"*

Instead of answering David looked her up and down and asked, *"Am I wrong?"*

Angela rolled her eyes and started down the stairs, leaving him where he was standing. He just knew he had ruined everything. Never in his life had a girl like Angela spoken to him unless she had to. He was kicking himself mentally when suddenly she stopped on the stairs.

"You can walk me to the bus stop," she said over her shoulder and winked back at him.

"Why you playin'?" David said, relieved, and bounded down the stairs after her.

When they reached the bus stop he looked around and saw that it didn't look like the bus was coming anytime soon. *"Um, I'll stay with you if you want me to. I don't want you to have to wait by yourself. This is kind of a bad neighborhood."*

"I'd like that," she said and smiled up at him. "I could use a man like you by my side to protect me."

David snapped back to reality and couldn't believe how different the woman before him was from the one he had met. The Angela he had met didn't care about what he had or what he could offer. She simply enjoyed his company and the fact that he had dreams. Money meant nothing to her and he would have bet millions that she would have stayed by his side if he only had a dime to his name. The Angela now would have left him so fast he wouldn't have even had the chance to begin counting to ten.

"I always thought you were out of my league," King David said. "I used to feel like I needed money and flashy things to impress you, but you didn't care about that back then. Or that is what you led me to believe, anyways. Now money is all you care about. We have so much of it that you would think we could find something better to talk about at lunch. So yes, Angela, please tell me. What happened? Or maybe this has always been the real you, and you've just chosen now to show the world your true colors."

Knowing that she would not have an answer, King David reached, grabbed his glass of Hennessy on the rocks, and took a sip.

Chapter 5

Detective Terrance Avery paced back and forth in his office trying to figure out where he had gone wrong in his plan. His feet had touched every inch of his office as he threatened to wear a hole in the bottom of his Stacy Adams. He tried hard to understand and put his finger on his mistake. He just didn't understand how he let his opportunity slip away.

"I had that motherfucker right where I wanted him!" he shouted to nobody in particular. "That motherfucker calls himself King. I'll show you what a king does!"

He went to his desk and flipped all of the loose-leaf paper up in the air and knocked everything else off of it. He had just gotten the news that the star witness in his investigation of David Mason, otherwise known as King David, had gone missing. Antonio Lesley had proven to be a key part of his whole investigation when he was picked up during a routine traffic stop. In his possession

Antonio had a kilo of heroin; and, at first when they brought him in, he was tough cookie to crack. He wanted so badly to prove his loyalty; however, when he was informed of how much time he was facing, he started singing like a bird. Detective Avery soon learned that Antonio was nothing but a shooter and a runner for none other than the notorious King David Mason. Detective Avery assured Antonio that as long as he complied with the law then all the charges against him would be dropped and he wouldn't have to worry about missing any time away from his beloved family. He was to wear a wire whenever he conducted business, and report back to Detective Avery once a week.

Everything was going good until one night when he went on a date with Davita Mason. At first Detective Avery was against it, but the more he thought about it the more he figured it would be good for business. He was supposed to contact Detective Avery the moment he got home from his date and then deliver the recording device that he had taped to him. Detective Avery hoped that the recording would hold incriminating evidence of the illegal dealings of her father's business. However, that was the last day anyone heard from Antonio. Their trace stopped at the restaurant where the two went to dine.

After sending some men there to investigate, Detective Avery was informed that the wire was found in the Dumpster behind the establishment. He called Antonio's phone back to back but received no answer; it went straight to voicemail every time.

Detective Avery wasn't naïve; he knew that if somehow it had come to be known that he was working with the law then there was slim chance to none that the kid was still alive. He knew his whole investigation had just blown up in his face and if, in fact, King David did know that he was being watched then all of his moves would be sharp.

"Dammit!" Detective Avery brought his closed black fists down on the wooden top of his desk before reaching for the landline in his office. He dialed a number and waited for the officer under him to answer. "Reese, I need you to go book Davita Mason right now."

"Davita Mason?" the officer responded and Detective Avery heard the stall in his voice. "Book her on account of what?"

"She is a suspect in a murder investigation. Find her and get her here now!"

Detective Avery didn't wait for Officer Reese to respond; he just slammed the phone down and went to take a seat behind his desk. He didn't care how much pull the Masons thought they had in St. Louis. They had plagued the city long enough and it was his job to take them down.

"Soooo, how did your date with Mr. Handsome go?"

Day sat in the salon chair at Blessings, the celebrity salon that her family owned, and waited for her nosey hair dresser to put the finishing touches on her blow out and flat iron. She popped the spearmint gun that she was chewing as she examined the shiny pink on her freshly manicured nails. A part of her wanted to roll her eyes when Jes asked the question but she should have known what would happen when she let it slip that she had a date in the first place.

"Mr. Handsome was a lame," she finally responded. "All these niggas here are lames and I'm starting to lose hope of ever meeting anyone on my level."

"On your level?" Jes giggled, snipping away at any split end she could find on Day's head. "Girl, you are too young to be worried about finding somebody on your level, okay?"

"Right!" Shonda, a chubby hairdresser, said from where she stood a couple of feet away. She was in the middle of putting highlights in an older woman's hair. "Sit up for me, baby, thank you. But anyways, Day, Jes is right! Girl, you too young to be out here tryin'a find love. The men you like are your age, which means mentally they are five years behind you. They aren't done playing games in these streets! So you better live your life, girl."

"See, that's why I knew I shouldn't have said nothin!" Day smacked her lips and rolled her eyes, causing Jes to yank a strand of hair from her head. "Ow! Jes! What was that for?"

"I ain't ya mama," Jes said and thumped Day's shoulder with her finger. "You not gon' get smart with me, girl."

Day couldn't help but to smile. Although very nosey, Jes was the only woman who had ever laid a finger on Day's head since she was a very small child. She had come to look at her like an aunt, and growing up Jes was always the one there to give her any advice she needed. The two had a bond that nobody would ever understand, but that was okay. Day talked her father into letting Jes manage the salon and putting her on salary. He would always tell her that he didn't understand the bond they had, but he was glad she had it with somebody.

"You ain't have to hit me, though! Or pull my hair out!"

"I grew this shit out, so I can do as I please. Shonda, you remember when this child first sat down in my chair? Oooh, Lawd! Hair was so nappy I probably cut my fingers a few times! And don't let me get started on them edges!"

By then everybody, including Day, was doubled over, laughing. Day couldn't be upset; she'd seen the pictures from when she was younger, and thanked God every day that her mother had stopped trying to style her hair.

"You know that's the reason your daddy even opened this shop, don't you?"

"I kind of had an idea." Day smiled up at Jes. "Some days I really love you, and some days—"

"Some days what, girl?" Jes said, making a face and cocking her head. She then put one hand on her hip and held up the scissors in her other hand. "Because I got these scissors and that flat iron is still hot, so you can pick your poison."

Day respected Jes so she didn't finish what she was about to say; instead, she just shook her head.

"Uh-huh, that's what I thought," Jes said. "Now tell me the real scoop on this 'lame' as you like to call him."

Before Day had a chance to respond there was a loud "ding," letting them know that someone had just entered the shop. Out of habit all eyes went to the front glass door and the shop instantly got quiet as if a plague had just walked in. Two white officers completely in uniform stood there glaring around at all of them. One was tall and skinny with red hair, while the other was short and stocky with blond. They didn't say anything at first, so Jes cleared her throat. "Can I help you?"

"We are here looking for a Davita Mason. You seen her?"

Instinctively Jes placed a firm hand on Day's shoulder and glared right on back at the officers. "What you want with her?"

"She is wanted in connection to a murder," the redhead said.

"Murder? Murdered who?" Jes exclaimed and grabbed Day's purse from Day's chair and placed it on a shelf behind her own body.

"It's cool, Jes," Day said up at her and removed the hand gently from her shoulder. She then spoke to the officers and nonchalantly put a finger in the air. "I'm Davita Mason. So I take it you're here to book me, huh?"

The officers wasted no time walking to where she was, where they yanked her up from the seat so that they could put her in cuffs. Day snatched her shoulder away from them because they were handling her so roughly for no reason and like she was a man.

"Now you mothafuckas hold on one minute! This here shop has cameras so you best think twice about how you handle her! Stop grabbing her like that dammit!"

The officers paid Jes no mind and continued as they pleased. Once they had Day in cuffs they pushed her forcefully to the doors, reading her all of her rights.

"Jes, call my daddy!" Day yelled right before the glass door shut.

The roughness didn't stop there. They threw her in the back seat of the police vehicle and did not bother strapping her in the way they were legally obligated to. Day being Day sat in the back and talked her mess the entire ride to the precinct.

"Y'all must not know who I am, huh?" She chuckled. "Stupid mothafuckas. Don't worry, though, I'll get your names and pass them along."

The redheaded officer turned his head so that he could look back at where she sat with her hands cuffed behind her back. He eyed her through the bars that separated them.

"Is that a threat, bitch?" he growled and turned up his lip. "In my world nobody gives a fuck about who your daddy is."

Day stared back into his eyes so coldly she saw him waver.

"I swear to God it is," she told him icily. "In my world my niggas don't give a fuck about them badges. We paint them mothafuckas every day."

The officer swallowed the lump in his throat and turned quickly back to the front. He had heard rumors of the terrible things that David Mason had done; he didn't know why he thought his daughter would be any different. They were, after all, booking her for murder. He was more than happy to get to the precinct so that he could go on about his day.

When they walked her to the interrogation room and removed her cuffs, she whipped around to face them. Instead of looking them in the face, her eyes went straight to their badges. She smirked before taking a seat and calmly clasping her hands together on top of the table like a schoolgirl. The officers looked at each other for a moment, already knowing what had just happened. They had heard that King David was the devil, and they were certain that they had just met his spawn.

When they left Day suddenly remembered the way Jes smoothly had removed her purse from the chair so the police wouldn't bring it with them. Jes had been around for a long time; she had seen a lot and done a lot. Day was almost positive that she was clearing the prepaid phone of all of its contents and was about to toss it that very moment. Day also was mentally preparing herself for the verbal lashing she would get for carrying around an unregistered weapon in broad daylight. Jes knew a little of Day's life, but what Day hadn't told her was that since she graduated she had been putting in work for her father. Day figured that if one day she would be a head of the table she might as well break herself in. She had always been cutthroat, and being heartless came easy, especially with a mother like hers. Since Angela always doted over David Jr. like he was some kind of golden statue, Day took to clinging to her father. Without knowing it she had become almost an exact replica of him and she saw the bigger picture that David Jr. didn't.

Although born with a silver spoon in her mouth Day always took the time to hang out in every hood spot she could find. She lived and breathed the street life and her friends would often joke and say that she was like New New from the movie *ATL*. She knew where her father came from and she related to that life more than the sheltered one her mother tried to force upon her. David Jr. went to private schools from elementary all the way to high school but Day refused. When she was about to enter high school she begged her father to put her in public school so that she would be able to view life the way normal kids did. She smiled to herself, remembering the conversation between her and her parents.

"Public school? Seriously, David! You're going to let our child go to public school? I thought all of this hard work was so our children would never have to go back to the hood!"

The family sat in the living room of their home having a debate. David Jr. and Davita sat next to each other with paperwork from their middle school. The papers needed to be turned in the next day so that the enrollment process into their high school of choice could be started.

"This is her decision, Angela. She will be protected."

"Okay, and what about in class if she gets into a fight? We went to those schools. You know those kids are savages. You know better than me."

"Mom," Davita said calmly. "I'm a teenager. That's what we do. We fight. Plus, I got these hands so you don't have anything to worry about."

David chuckled and nodded approvingly at his daughter's response. Angela looked taken aback for a moment before turning to glare at her husband.

"Do you see how she talks? Like some ghetto girl from the streets!"

"Mom, you're dragging it out! I don't want to be all preppy like your nerdy son right here. I want to be normal!"

"I am normal, stupid." David Jr. jumped at her.

"Barely." Davita rolled her eyes. "Daddy, will you sign my paper, please? You went to public school and now you're rich. I feel like no matter where I go to school I will be following in good footsteps."

King David took her paper and smirked when he saw that she had chosen the exact same high school he and her mother went to.

"Good choice," he said and signed the paper. He then looked at his wife. "One day you have to accept the fact that she is not like you. She will be okay."

The sound of a door slamming snapped Day from memory lane. She didn't jump; she just looked up to see who was in a bad mood.

She didn't recognize the tall dark-skinned man. She gave him a once-over and analyzed his hard face, low-cut hair, and cheap blue suit. *Rat.* Day hated the police, especially black officers simply because she felt that they were sellouts. They turned their backs on their own people and culture just to please a white face that really didn't care if they lived or died.

Her face rested but her eyes were hard and when his reached hers, they matched. It was her first time ever in an interrogation room but she'd seen movies and read books. Above her the light flickered and she knew that was a tactic they used to make their victims nervous. It wasn't working. In his hands the detective carried nothing, no folder, no papers. So that let Day know that she was there off of speculation. She smirked.

"Is something funny to you, Ms. Mason?" Detective Avery asked and took a seat on the opposite side of the table.

"Nooope," Day responded childishly. "How are you today, Detective?"

"I would be better if I didn't have to deal with scum niggas like you on a day-to-day basis."

"Ouch." Day pretended to wince but then came back at him. "I would be better if I didn't have to see sellouts like you patrolling the streets. Rat. Does it hurt? You know, when they fuck you in the ass?"

"Oh, trust me," Detective Avery said, "it's going to hurt much worse when I fuck you in the ass. Now tell me, Ms. Mason, where were you three nights ago?"

"Three nights ago?"

"Come on now, Ms. Mason, I know that inside of that beautiful head of yours you must have a brain that can comprehend the simplest of questions, right?"

"Three nights ago, hmm, let's see." Day pretended to think. "Oh, yeah. I went on a date with this lame. His name was Terrance . . . Tommy . . ."

"Tony," Detective Avery corrected her.

"Tony!" Day snapped her fingers. "That's it."

"You went on a date with Antonio Lesley, and now he's dead and we have reason to believe that it was you who killed him. You were the last person who was seen with him and video footage from that restaurant shows you walking out with him."

Day knew that was the part where most people incriminated themselves by talking too much, so she sat there quiet for a moment. She knew that there was no way that the detective could know for sure if Tony was dead because his body was in a place that he couldn't be found. Instead she just cocked her head and squinted her eyes.

"You don't look too surprised." He leaned back in his seat. "Why is that?"

"The impression that I got from Tony was that he liked to play around in the streets. A lot of niggas who like to play in the streets end up dead. That doesn't mean I killed him. You should know that."

Detective Avery stared at her, slightly irritated that she hadn't bought his bluff. He tapped his fingers on the table and decided his next course of action. "When is the last time you saw Antonio Lesley? Alive or dead."

"The last time I saw Tony was when I left that restaurant."

"Did he take you home?"

"We came and left in two separate cars," Day lied without missing a beat. She was almost positive that the restaurant didn't have cameras all the way to the parking lot, and if they did she hoped they were just for show. "You know I would call my lawyer, but I don't think I need to. Do you have any evidence tying me to the murder besides the fact that he and I went to dinner, you know, something that young people do? Why aren't you out in the streets trying to figure out who murdered this man? Did he get shot, stabbed? Shit, did he get strangled? And why now all of a sudden is the police department so worried about the death of a black street runner?"

The two connected eyes and Day had the hardest fight within herself to hold the smile threatening to plague her face. She knew he knew why Tony ended up dead. Because he was a snitch, but she wasn't going to say that. Playing dumb was her best bet.

"You, Ms. Mason," Detective Avery said and turned his nose up at her, "are full of shit. I can see it in your eyes."

"That's cool and everything but I feel like you're wastin' my time right now, Detective Amos."

"Avery!"

"Yeah, yeah. Whatever. Am I being arrested?"

When he didn't say anything, which she knew he wouldn't, she stood to her feet and nodded her head at him. "I take that as a no," she said and swung her long, natural hair over her shoulder as she made her way to the door.

"I'll be seeing you again," Detective Avery warned. "Soon."

"I'm used to niggas stalking me." Day winked at him not thinking twice to entertain his warning. "So that's cool."

Chapter 6

The watcher sat inside of the black Escalade and, through tinted windows, eyed him getting into his Mercedes-Benz. Mixed emotions plagued inside but still it was too early to make a move. Yet the time to exact revenge was coming nearer and nearer.

Do it now! the watcher's mental screamed.

"No! Not yet. Soon though. Very soon," the watcher said out loud although nobody was in the vehicle with them.

The watcher had been keeping tabs on David Mason Jr. for the last couple of weeks, taking notice of his habits and the people who he liked to be around, and getting used to his routine. He was interesting, nothing like his cold-hearted father, but still Mason blood ran through him. Which meant he would have to pay.

Chapter 7

The sound of running water filled the kitchen and the smell of the roast slow cooking in the Crock-Pot on the counter invaded Angela's nostrils. She inhaled deeply and listened to her family in the other room having basic chitchat. It was the first time in weeks that they had all been under the same roof together and she wasn't sure yet if it was a blessing or a curse. After her solo dinner with her husband she had been very standoffish with everyone, including her son. The dinner that night hadn't even been set up by her; David had put it together. As always, everyone had to be on his time. When he was expected to be on theirs he was a no-show.

She sighed deeply and walked to the island in her kitchen to grab her wineglass and take a sip. She didn't even know what the name of the wine was; she just knew that it cost $2,000 and in her mind the price made it ten times better. After she guzzled down the glass Angela wiped the corners of her lips and made her way into the dining room. The first sight she saw at the table meant for six was, of course, Davita smiling ear to ear and having a conversation with her father. The next was David Jr. with his head bent down and his eyes on his phone and his fingers moving. She took her seat at the other end of the table and smiled in her son's direction. Both of her children were a perfect blend of her and her husband, but David Jr. had her smile. He felt his mother's eyes on him and he looked up at her, returning her smile.

"Hey, Ma, the food smells good," he said. "Why you always gotta cook, though? Don't got money for cooks and shit?"

"Watch your mouth," Angela responded to him, smoothing out the tablecloth in front of her. "And because when my whole family is here I would like my hands to be the ones that prepare the food that you guys eat."

"Poison," Day coughed into her hand and King David shot her a look, although it seemed as if he was holding back a laugh.

He wanted them all to have a peaceful dinner and in a sense he wanted to make his absence up to his family. Things weren't perfect among them and he felt that he had been bringing his cold heart into his home. He and Day had a tight bond but their family consisted of four. However, when it came to Angela he already knew that money was the only thing she cared about at that point in time. He could blame her, but in all actuality it was his fault. During the years that they had been married he had become more and more distant. Not because he wanted to be, but that is what happens when a man builds an empire. He had to put in the work to get to where he needed to be and while he was putting in that work the only comfort Angela had was in the money he gave her to spend. At the time he thought he was making up for him being gone, when what he was really doing was creating a monster.

When it came to David Jr. he didn't know how to relate to him the way he related to Davita. Ever since David Jr. was little he stayed underneath his mother so his mindset was not entirely his fault. King David would never knock his son for wanting to get his education, but he did not like the fact that he was barely willing to learn about his roots. He didn't like the fact that he refused to pay homage to the reason he wasn't just like the people he turned his nose up at. David Jr. needed to understand that if his father hadn't done everything he had done, illegal or not, they would be living in some two-bedroom apartment in the hood. He wouldn't have had the privilege to go to all the fancy schools that his mother had sent him to. He wouldn't have the clothes that he wore, nor would he have been able to drive a different vehicle every year since the day he got his license.

King David sat there tapping his index finger on the tablecloth, and stared at his son and wife making small talk before he decided to cut in. "How has school been, son?"

Shocked, David Jr. stopped talking instantly when he heard his father's voice. "It's been good," David Jr. responded, giving his dad an awkward look. "Why you ask?"

"Just wanna know how my son is," King David said. "We don't talk much these days."

"Yeah, maybe because you're too busy in the streets being King David."

"Or maybe because you're too busy trying not to be David Jr."

To that David Jr. had no response because he had to admit his father was right. He submerged himself in his studies so as not to be swayed by the street life. The most he had been doing for his father was going in and making sure his counts were right, since his old financial advisor had quit on him. Other than that David Jr. didn't indulge himself too much in anything that his father had going on.

"The food should be done," Angela said a little too evenly, and King David could tell that she must have had a couple of glasses of wine to drink.

When she exited he turned his attention back to his son. Across from David Jr. Day had leaned back in her seat, knowing that things were about to get more than just a little bit juicy. David Jr. cleared his throat once his mother was gone and opened his mouth to speak.

"I just want to make my own way," David Jr. said. "Is that a crime?"

"Yes, it's a crime, fool," Day chimed in before her father could say a word. "I don't know why you're bustin' your ass for a job that you only going to make three hundred bands a year for. Nigga, you're already sittin' on a gold mine!"

"If I wanted to I could, but I want to do something different with my life."

"If you wanted to you could?" King David's eyes had never left his son's. "You don't have it in you to take my place." He smirked at David Jr., taunting him. He was pleased when he saw his son's expression change and he saw that the insult had done something.

"How do you figure I don't?"

"Because you're ungrateful. You have done everything in your power to shun me. You don't have it in you because wouldn't do for your family what I have done for mine."

"I wouldn't have to."

"Exactly. I made sure of that."

Once again David Jr. was at a loss for words. He had no rebuttal and he felt the side of his face grow warm as Day burned a hole into it with her glare.

She couldn't believe that he kept smiting their father the way that he did. She never understood why he was so withdrawn from the family business. In all their years she had never even seen him look at a gun, let alone touch one. She sneered in his direction and curled her top lip. "Daddy, I don't even know why you waste your time. This nigga wouldn't last a day on the streets. Nerdy-ass boy."

"Just because I don't tote pistols around like a wallet doesn't mean I wouldn't bust one," David Jr. lied through his teeth, annoyed that his sister had just tried to play him like a punk.

They had both been raised in the same type of environment. It was true to say that David Jr. had never taken a life; however, if it came down to it he would definitely throw hands. After he made his comment he looked back at his father. Something in him said that he had just made a big mistake and when King David spoke he knew he was correct for the assumption.

"Prove it."

"What?"

"Yeah," Day instigated. "You sayin' basically that you're in school by choice and not because you're scared of the streets, right? So prove it, college boy."

King David clasped his hands together but left his index fingers pointed upward at the ceiling. The smirk was still on his face and it was driving David Jr. crazy. Although his mental was screaming for him not to do it, the last thing he needed was his father, the king of St. Louis, thinking he was a little bitch. He didn't want that rep in the streets and, no matter how much he wanted to walk his own path, he didn't want to be disowned, especially since he knew he was in his father's will somewhere.

"A'ight," he said. "When?"

"Tonight," King David said without thinking twice. "After dinner you both will ride with me. I had something I was going to call some little niggas to handle, but I have two of my own right in front of me."

At that moment Angela waltzed back in from the kitchen, carrying trays of food and placing them on the table. She instantly noticed the different type of vibe in the air and when her eyes reached her son's face she could tell something was off. It held no expression and no emotion. Day, on the other hand, had a smug look on her face, like she had just won the lottery. Shrugging it off, Angela just guessed that Day must have just gotten under his skin again with her words like she always did.

"You scared, huh?" Day laughed at her brother's discomfort. She could tell that he wished that he'd just kept his mouth shut.

"I ain't never scared," David Jr. responded evenly and started to load his plate with food.

"Yeah, right," Day scoffed while she also piled food on her plate. "You ain't never put in no work."

Although she was feeling a buzz, Angela whipped her head to David Jr. "Put in work? What is she talking about?"

"Don't worry about it, Ma," David Jr. tried to brush it off. "We are just going to handle some business with Dad after dinner."

"What?" Angela turned to glare at King David. "My son is not some street thug!"

King David sat there wearing a black Versace button-up that accented his muscular frame. His hair was freshly lined up and the golden Rolex on his wrist gleamed from the chandelier above them. Although he was in his mid-forties he did not have a wrinkle in his smooth brown

skin nor did he have a gray hair on his head.
He was sitting there looking very delectable;
however, that was the last thing on Angela's
mind. At home her husband was just David to
her, but that didn't change the fact that he would
murder in cold blood if he had to. Same with
Davita. She didn't want that for David Jr. She
wanted something else.

"David Jr.—"

"Wants to prove himself." King David stared
icily into his wife's eyes, reminding her of the
request she made at dinner the other night. "He
wants to show us that he isn't scared of the
streets."

"It is already apparent that he isn't afraid of
them." Angela's voice was soft and sharp. "He
has you for a father. I don't understand why you
would want to create another monster."

"You married this monster. No, I'm sorry, I
forgot. You married my money," King David's
deep voice barked. "You want for him to have
more shares? Then he needs to prove himself. I
love my children but I'm not leaving my empire
to a pussy nigga, even if it is my son. Now let's
eat."

Angela knew that there was nothing else she
could say on the topic. Her eyes darted to Day,
who instantly looked down at her plate, then

to David Jr., who just shook his head at her. She sighed because she knew she was fighting a losing battle. The last thing she needed was for her son to get killed trying to follow in his father's misguided footsteps. When she looked at her husband, he was still looking at her with a small smile on his face.

"I'm going to get some more wine." She excused herself, rolling her eyes.

David Jr. sat on the full-sized bed of his old bedroom, letting his palms smooth out the old blue comforter. He looked around the room and felt a rush of emotion come over him. Growing up in his parents' house had never been easy for him; he always felt like the black sheep of the family. Yet whenever he was in his room, his own space, everything seemed to make sense to him. That room had provided him peace when he had none. On the walls were posters of many black icons such as Martin Luther King Jr., Malcom X, and President Barack Obama. They always made him feel like he was in the presence of greatness. His eyes wandered to the desktop computer on a desk in the far corner that looked like it hadn't been used for years.

"Hunh," a voice said, interrupting his thought process. He looked up and saw that it was his sister in the doorway throwing something at him. "All black. You ready?"

The fabric landed on his lap and David Jr. could see that it was an all-black hoodie. He didn't hesitate to put it on, and bent down to make sure his black Timberland boots were tied. Looking back up at his sister he saw that she, too, wore an all-black hoodie, thick black leggings, and a pair of all-black Burberry boots.

"Yeah, I'm ready."

The time read just after midnight when the two piled into Day's all-black Chevy Camaro; and David Jr. was slightly shocked when they pulled off without waiting for their father. He assumed that he must have gone ahead of them. Davita nodded her head to the glove compartment, telling him to open it.

"The burners are in there," she said and, sure enough, when he opened it there were two chrome .45s staring back at him. He grabbed them and handed one to her. "You don't even have your own gun, do you, David Jr.?"

"What do I need a gun for?"

Day looked at her brother like he was stupid. "Because you are the son of St. Louis's kingpin. Nigga, just because Daddy be having all these goons around us all the time don't mean that you can't be caught slippin'. The game has changed. These niggas be out here wildin'. When we're done here keep that gun with you."

"I'm cool," he said, placing the gun in his lap.

That irritated Day. She looked at him like she wanted to smack him. She never understood how the two of them were twins. They weren't the same in any way, and if he weren't her brother she was positive that she wouldn't communicate with him at all.

"Are you stupid? Like, why do you gotta act all uppity all the time? You and Mom act like y'all don't know where y'all come from!"

"She isn't from the streets. And we weren't born in the hood, either. In case you forgot."

On that note Day jerked the car on the side of the interstate and pressed hard on the brakes, causing David Jr. to lurch forward. She turned her whole body to face him and tried hard to fight the urge to punch him in his handsome face.

"These are our roots nigga. Our building blocks. Never forget. You wanna get comfortable and lose everything? I'm out here putting in work for you. That's what you get for always being under ya mama's titty instead of being out in the real world like me. You got the skin of a black man, but the mentality of a white mothafucka."

"Putting in work for me? You ain't never did shit for me," he told her and turned his eyes to the front of the car again.

Day's gaze on his face was fiery and she shook her head at her brother. He was so naïve. The ones he brushed off were the only ones who really had his back. He thought he was alone but he wasn't. He was never alone, not even when he was at school. Every security guard hired at the school was on their father's payroll. Some of the students on campus weren't even really students and any day that he had class the entire building was surrounded with experienced shooters. Despite any disagreements between the father and son, King David always kept a couple of eyes on him and stayed distant at the same time. Instead of pointing all of that out to him Day just faced forward and put a hand on the gear shift.

"Do you remember last year when your updated scholarship information came late?" Her voice was soft as she spoke to, but didn't look at, her brother. "It actually came on time."

"What?" David Jr. asked, confused, glancing over her way.

"The first one came on time, anyway. I was nosey so I opened it." She paused and chuckled. "It said that they had revoked your entire scholarship because you failed that math class, remember?" She clenched her jaw and shook her head. "They took all your funds away over one class, when you had straight As in all of your others. That was crazy to me, just another way for the white man to keep the black man down. And I know you, David Jr. You wouldn't have asked Daddy for the money. Even if it was your last year of school. Since you try so hard to show him that you don't need him."

David Jr. sat there in silence. All he remembered was getting a letter in the mail saying that he had gotten more money toward his college education. He also remembered getting his grades back and seeing that the math course he had failed was nowhere even on the listing. He opened his mouth to ask a question but she beat him to the punch.

"I put a burner to the dean's temple and explained to him all of the reasons why it was in his best interest to delete that grade from the system and make sure you kept your scholarship. And now here we are: me, still a savage in your eyes, and you? Still a uppity-ass nigga in mine."

The only thing that could be heard was the purring of the engine as her words played in David Jr.'s head. He didn't know what to say at first. The two had never really gotten along.

"Why would you do that?" he finally asked.

"Because you're my brother, stupid." Without saying another word Day pulled back into the interstate traffic and David Jr. didn't say a thing the rest of the ride to their destination.

It took almost forty-five minutes to get to the address Day had scribbled down on a piece of paper. When they pulled onto a street in Fountain Park, Day slowed the car and glanced down at the paper one more time before pointing her finger.

"That's the house right there," she told him and parked the car three houses down from the one she had pointed at. "Here, put this on. Niggas be snitching these days."

She tossed over to him a black face mask with the eyes and mouth cut out, and he stared blankly down at it. She didn't wait for him to put his on before she pulled hers down on her own face. She unbuckled her seat belt and grabbed her weapon up from her lap so that she could check the clip. From the corner of her eye she saw David Jr. put on his face mask, and when he did that she reached in the pockets of her hoodie and pulled out two sets of leather black gloves.

"Hunh." She handed one of the pairs to him. "Put these on, too. Check your clip and then we can go."

"Where is Dad?" David Jr. asked after checking his clip and seeing that it was full.

Day grabbed a black duffle bag from the back seat before she opened her car door and looked back at her brother with a smirk. "Dad ain't coming. He's back at the house." She knew that underneath his mask his expression was of pure shock. He didn't know that it would be just him and Day.

"What?"

"The perks of being the king," Day said, shutting her car door and waiting for David Jr. to follow suit. "You have little niggas who will handle your lightweight while you sleep. Come on, let's get this shit over with."

David Jr. didn't know what he had gotten himself into. He thought that his dad would be there to oversee things just in case they went bad; he was wrong. He should have never let his ego get the best of him at the dinner table because he could be back at home in his condo right then. He was nervous because the only place that he had ever shot a gun at was the gun range. And although he had incredible aim there, those were still targets.

He fixed the mask on his face and couldn't help but to notice that it smelled like the perfume he'd gotten Day for Christmas the year before. Holding the gun tightly in his right hand, he followed his sister as she half walked, half ran to the brick house. The spring night was cool and the fact that they wore black blended them in well with the shadows. Before they even reached the house they could hear the music booming from it and loud laughter. From the sounds of it the habitants were having some kind of party. When they finally reached the house, Day looked at her brother and prepped him.

"We're going through the front door?"

"I'm a gangster. I don't gotta break into no-body's crib. We're here to collect a debt. We get in, get the money, and leave. Got it?"

David Jr. nodded his head and asked, "What if they don't have the money?"

"If they don't, then we are the only ones who will ever leave this house again. Get ready, and don't be scared. Just back me up. You're the prince. You run shit. Remember that."

Without wasting another moment Day knocked on the door and stepped to the side, and David Jr. did the same.

"Who is it?" a gruff voice yelled from the other side.

"Boy, stop playin'! You know it's me," Day called out in a sweet voice.

When the door opened she didn't even give the man a chance to look outside before swinging her fist and connecting with his nose. When he was knocked back she rushed in the house with David Jr. close behind her. Before the man could get back up she kicked him in his temple, knocking him out cold. She quickly analyzed her surroundings and fired her gun in the air, shocking everyone in the house. The house was one story and from the looks of it everyone was having a party in the living room of the place. There were four big, bulky men, including the one she had knocked down, and four half-naked white women. On the coffee table Day saw white lines and it seemed that they were in the middle of taking them. As soon as the women saw the armed, masked intruders enter the house they started screaming at the top of their lungs.

"What the fuck?" one of the men said and boldly stood to his feet. He didn't know who the hell they thought they were, busting into his house like the feds. "Do you know who the fuck I am?"

David instinctively pointed his gun to the living room and took notice that all the men were armed.

"I don't give a fuck who you are, my nigga," Day said, also pointing her gun at the man. "It's all about who I am. King David wants his money."

The man before her was tall and heavyset. His hair was cut low and his sideburns led into his mustache and beard. He looked at the small frame before him and matched it with the voice. He burst out laughing before he could control himself.

"So this is how King James does his business? He got bitches shooting for him now?"

"Are you Big Mike?" Day asked, ignoring his comment.

"No, bitch, I—"

Bang! Day fired her gun once and shot him in the center of his forehead. The back of his head exploded and the blood and brain particles sprayed on the women behind him before he dropped lifelessly to the ground.

"Fuck is you talking for then?" Day growled and turned back to the last two men on the couch. She eyed them and saw that one had the name MIKE tattooed on his arm, and she focused on him. He had dark brown eyes and cornrows in his hair. "You niggas are wasting my time, but even more you are wasting King David's. You have three options: give me money or give me the drugs."

"What's the third option?" Big Mike said, trying to hide the fact that he was shook that little mama had just bodied his partner like it was nothing.

"Give me your soul." She cocked her gun back and aimed it at his head.

"A'ight! A'ight!" Big Mike put his hands in the air. "I got the money! It's in the basement, though."

Day eyed him suspiciously before looking back at her brother and nodding her head. "Go with him and make sure all twenty-five thousand is accounted for. Especially since these niggas wanna be up here getting high with bitches."

David Jr. nodded his head and waved his gun. "Come on," he said to Big Mike.

Big Mike stood up from the couch and led David Jr. to the basement. David Jr. kept his gun pointed at his head the whole way down the stairs. The basement was laid out nicely, with red carpets, leather couches, and big-screen TVs.

"Over there." Big Mike pointed to a safe behind the bar.

"Go get it," David Jr. said. "And don't try no funny shit."

Big Mike nodded as he walked, and then began putting in the code to open the safe. He chuckled and shook his head at the kid behind him. "You ain't never did this shit before, huh?"

David Jr. ignored the comment. He just threw the duffle bag at him once the safe was open.

"I can tell just by the way you holdin' that gun, boy. You don't even look like you've even busted a gun at a real person before. You scared?"

"Fuck I got to be scared about, nigga?" David Jr. asked. "I'm the one with the gun."

Big Mike chuckled again. "Wrong." The sudden sound of a gun cocking filled the air in the basement.

David Jr. was caught off guard when Big Mike whipped around and pointed a black firearm at him. With only a split second to react he squeezed the trigger and caught Big Mike in the neck. But he didn't stop shooting his gun until it started clicking. He had made Big Mike dance backward before he finally fell dead with a big thud to the ground. David Jr. inhaled deeply when he saw what he had just done. He didn't feel anything as he stared down into Big Mike's blank eyes. He let the gun fall loosely to his side and stood still for a second. Suddenly he felt somebody come from behind him and touch his arm gently.

"Go get the money," he heard his sister's voice say.

When Day looked at Big Mike lying dead on the floor the only thing she paid attention to was the gun still being held tightly in his hand.

"Damn, this nigga had a gun in his safe?" She walked over and grabbed the gun that her brother had while he was loading the cash in the duffle bag. "You was scared."

"How you figure?" David Jr. asked and zipped the bag up.

She grabbed his gun and showed him the clip. "You emptied your clip close range."

"Nah, not scared," David Jr. said and stepped over Big Mike to head back to the stairs. The blood spilling out of his body matched the red carpet perfectly. "Insulted. Take me home."

Chapter 8

The birds chirping outside of his window didn't bother David Jr., mostly because he was already awake. After Day had dropped him off he took a long, hot shower and then tried to go to sleep. However, sleep couldn't find him. He couldn't stop thinking about the way Day had taken a life so effortlessly. It was almost like it didn't mean anything to her, like she was unmoved by it. When she had seen what he had done to Big Mike he was sure that he saw a satisfied look in her eyes. She was pleased. Her brother wasn't a pussy after all. He was sure she'd already taken the news back to their father.

He was lying on his back and staring at his ceiling, trying to get his thoughts together. He tried to make himself feel sad about taking that man's life, but whenever he would start to feel remorse it was replaced with anger instead. He remembered the things Big Mike had said about him and he also knew that if he hadn't shot first then he would be dead. He had to do it, and that realization alone made him sick to his stomach.

He was still lost in his thoughts when his phone started to vibrate on the oak wood nightstand beside his bed. He picked it up and saw that it was a message from his father, telling him to meet him for lunch in an hour. He sighed and tossed the phone back down. A split second later it began to vibrate again. When he picked it up that time he saw a number that he did not recognize pop up on the screen.

"Hello?" he said into the receiver.

"Hey, I didn't know if you would be up or not." The soft voice sounded familiar but he couldn't put a face to it.

"Who this?" he asked.

"You don't recognize my voice? It's Indigo. Remember me?"

That made David Jr. sit straight up in his bed and clear his throat. "Aw, my bad. What's up? How'd you get my number?."

"I have my ways," she said jokingly. "Honestly, I wasn't going to call you," she admitted on the other end, "but then I saw this movie on Lifetime about second chances and decided to give you one."

"For real?"

"Nah, I'm bullshitting you." She laughed. "But the last time I saw you, you looked like a sad puppy dog, and I haven't been able to get your face out of my head since."

"I knew these handsome features of mine would be of use one day." David Jr. grinned to himself, putting all of his negative thoughts to the back of his mind.

"Or maybe I just felt sorry for you."

"Damn, like that?" David laughed. "Well, either way, I'll take it. What do you have planned for the day? Can I see you?"

"Umm, sure," she said skeptically.

"I promise I won't kidnap you. What about tonight? We can go to dinner; and my dad owns this club. We can stop by there if you want." David Jr. didn't remember the last time he had asked a girl on a date. Most of the time women would just be at the parties he attended and would end up in his bed. The words felt awkward coming from his mouth.

"Okay, that sounds cool. Just text me and let me know what time and stuff. Cool?"

"A'ight, coo'."

"What are you about to do right now?"

"Shit." Davis Jr. stood up and stretched. "Just go meet my dad at Ruth's Chris Steak House. He wants to talk."

"Oooh, sounds serious."

"Yeah, well. You know how that goes," David Jr. said, trying to make light of the topic.

"Uh-huh," Indigo said and then paused for a moment. "Well, I'll let you get ready, I won't hold you. Don't forget to text me."

"I won't," David Jr. reassured her before they disconnected the phone.

Indeed he wouldn't. She was just what he needed to take his mind off of the world around him.

King David sat alone at slightly packed restaurant as he waited for his son to join him. He wore a casual Armani cream button-up with tan slacks, which he had hiked up slightly to show off the cream Armani socks that matched his shirt. After Day came in the house by herself with the duffle bag of money he had of course inquired where David Jr. was. When she told him that he had requested to go home he knew he needed to meet with his son and pick his brain a little bit. It was time that David Jr. embrace who he was.

When he finally saw his son being led to the table by the host, he motioned to the chair on the opposite side of him.

"What's up, Dad," David Jr. greeted him. "You couldn't wait for me to order?" He nodded his head toward the steak already in front of his father.

"You couldn't be on time?"

"I had some things to handle," David Jr. lied. He honestly was late because he was contemplating not even going at all. He wasn't ready to face his father and he definitely wasn't ready to discuss anything that had happened the night before. He sat there and stared down at the Legend Blue retro Jordans on his feet, and rubbed his hands together. "So what's up?"

King David studied his son. He couldn't help smirking. It was almost like he was seeing himself young all over again. He had to admit that his son had much more style than he ever had, and he had much more luck with the ladies. He was also more arrogant and he didn't know how to control his hot temper, much like Day. However, that was not a trait that he wanted his son, a man, to have.

"Why didn't you come back to the house last night?"

"Because I have my own house."

"Touché." King David tilted his glass of water to his son before taking a swig. "You aren't going to order anything to eat?"

"Nah, I'm not hungry. So what's up, Dad? What you call me here for? You want to talk about last night or something?"

"Straight to the point I see," King David said and cut another piece of his steak. "I already know what happened last night so there is no need for us to discuss it."

"Then what? You called me here to watch you eat?"

"I called you here to talk about your position in the family business." King David looked square into David Jr.'s eyes. "This is your last year of school. You graduate in a couple of months. I let you do your thing; now it's time that I bring you back."

"What if that isn't what I want for myself?"

"After last night I thought you'd have changed your mind."

Shaking his head, David Jr. leaned forward and put his arms on the table. "If anything, it made me want to not have anything to do with this shit even more," he told his father. "If that's the shit you have to do then I'm good. You got Day out here running around like a nigga. We could have gotten killed last night. That's what you want for us? You want us out there like that?"

"You still don't get it, do you? Or do I need to call off every one of the bodies I have tailing you wherever you go so you can see just how many people will come for your head? You are here. You came from me. There is no place on this earth that you can go and not be King David's son. Understand that."

"I can still make my own way."

"And I can guarantee you that, when it is all said and done with, you will still end up on my side of the table. You are a Mason. There is no running from that. All that bullshit your mother put in your head got you out here acting all uppity, like you're better than everyone."

"You sound like Day." David Jr. leaned back in his chair.

"Sit up straight at my table," King David said in a low but deadly voice. When his son did as he was instructed, he continued, "Day is insulted by the way you treat her, and by the way you react to me. She knows this business like the back of her hand; and she can shoot. She's not scared and this is the life that she has come to know. But that doesn't make her a leader. That makes her a right hand. Yours. So the real question is, do you want her out there like that?"

"She don't fuck with me. Plus, I already have a right hand."

"Who, Roland? That nigga couldn't see himself to a door if it was right in front of him." King David put his fork down and focused on his son's face. "That's your problem. No matter what happens you ain't never supposed to put anybody before family. As much resentment that Davita has toward you, she would bust her gun first at anybody who threatened you. She would lay her life down for you, but would you do the same?"

David Jr. was quiet. After what Day had told him the night before about his scholarship, he had begun to wonder if she really didn't like him, or if it was just a show. Maybe it was always he who had pushed her away and not the other way around. He had always judged her for wanting to be a part of her father's business instead of wanting something better for herself. He never took the time to think that maybe this was the life that was best for her. He felt like shit, because he knew that everything his father was saying was true. David Jr. had tried so hard for years to not be like his father that he forgotten he was still King David's son at the end of the day. Mason blood coursed through his veins. It dawned on him at that very moment that he would never be able to get away from who he was. No matter how may schools he went to and no matter what job he got, he would always be a Mason.

"Yes," David Jr. said, shocking King David.

"Good," King David said and eyed his son curiously. "Your mother asked me to release more assets to you and at first I was against it. But then I started to think maybe it is my fault that you don't want anything to do with my business. I have released more than half of my assets to you. I have also removed your mother from my will and you will have everything that was once released to her."

"Why? Why would you remove Ma from your will?"

"Because she is not the woman I fell in love with," King David responded honestly. "She does not want you to be anything like me. At one point in time I was everything to her, or so I thought. If in you she sees me and despises it? I don't think she ever loved me at all. Why would I leave anything of mine to someone who looks down on the way I got it?"

"So then why would you leave it to me?"

"Because you don't really look down on it, or me." King David read his son. "I see the way your eyes light up whenever you come and do counts. You force yourself to stay away but now I think after last night you know. You know that there is no running from it. You, my son, have collected your first soul. Now you have no choice. Because, now, I have leverage."

"You gon' blackmail me to work for you?"

"Is it really blackmail if you do it willingly?"

David Jr. stared at his hands for a moment and thought about how he felt when he squeezed the trigger. He thought about the power he felt and the fact that he felt no regret; but still he wasn't completely sold.

"I ain't no street nigga," he said, and his words got a reaction.

"You are my son and I love you. Despite the things I did to build this empire, it's built, and I did it for you and your sister. I grew up fighting. I didn't have shit where I came from and when my mom died I had nowhere to go but the streets. I had to drop out of school because I had to eat and the streets fed me. If I cut you off right now where would you go?" King David couldn't help feeling slighted by his son's words. "Exactly. I named you after myself not so that you would have to live in my shadow, but so that your name would hold power. And so that you would never have to work as hard as me, just rule. And pass on our legacy. You say you ain't a street nigga, but I was. And look how far it got me. Now I'm the king, just like you will be. Kings never *have* to run the streets. We just go to meetings. Which brings me to the next topic."

When King David didn't continue David Jr. assumed he wanted him to ask, so he did. "What's that?"

"We have a very important meeting a week from Saturday. At one p.m. sharp."

"We?"

"We, as in you and me. You have a choice to make now. Either you come to the meeting with me and take your rightful place by my side, or . . ."

"Or what?" David Jr. inquired when his father's voice trailed off.

"Since you want to prove your independence so bad, you do just that. With no funds from me. No home, no car. I will cut you off and you will see exactly what it is like to be a street nigga."

The watcher viewed them as they exited Ruth's Chris Steak House, and then turned the key in the ignition. It was time. Seeing the two men embrace and say their goodbyes before they parted ways was almost sickening.

"Yeah, say your last goodbyes. You son of a bitch."

Go! Hurry up before you lose him!

"Shut up!" The watcher hated hearing the mental voice speak.

Pulling into traffic the Escalade stayed at least two cars behind the all-black Buick. Finally the Buick dropped him off in front of a club and he walked inside alone. Parking the Escalade, the watcher casually reached over to the passenger's seat and grabbed the 9 mm pistol and wrapped a hand around it. The watcher then reached into the glove compartment, grabbed a silencer from it, and screwed it on the gun. After concealing the weapon, the watcher stepped out of the vehicle and walked slowly toward the front door of the club. At that time of the day it was a restaurant and there were many people there dining in. Giving fake smiles to those passing, the watcher saw him get on an elevator, and then headed in that direction. Looking up at the lights, it was noted mentally that the elevator had stopped on the third floor. When it came back down the watcher got on and pressed the number three button out of all of the choices and hoped that he was there alone. However, even if he wasn't it wouldn't matter; nobody was going to make it back down the elevator.

Ding!

The elevator sounded when it reached its destination and, when he heard the elevator, King David turned around to see who had come up behind him. He had just opened the door to his office and he wasn't expecting anybody at that moment. When he saw who it was he held a look of confusion on his face.

"Remember me?" the watcher said and aimed the gun.

Pfft!

The bullet caught King David in his shoulder and knocked him back. When he went for his own gun at his waist he caught a bullet in his other shoulder. And another one in his gut. And two more in his legs.

"Augh!" he shouted out as he stumbled back into his office. He fell into one of the chairs on his desk. "Wh . . . who are you?"

"Your worst nightmare," the watcher said and walked slowly into the room, smiling. "Or your karma. Whichever one you want to call me I'm fine with."

The watcher walked into the room and set the pistol on the desk and listened to the sound of King David's blood dripping onto the carpet. Reaching in the pocket of their jeans the watcher pulled out two sets of brass knuckles and put them on.

"I don't know you," King David said, panting and trying to eat the pain from his wounds.

"Look closer!" the watcher said and got in his face. "Look in my eyes! Look at my face! Who am I?"

King David focused his eyes on the face in front of him and suddenly it dawned on him. The resemblance was uncanny. "You!"

"I am here as retribution for all of those who you crossed. For all you have killed. I am here to burn you empire to the ground! When I'm done with you, they won't even be able to recognize your body. Just like his."

The crunching sound of brass knuckles on bones and painful screams filled the air for hours to come.

Chapter 9

"I'm having a really good time!" Indigo shouted over the loud music inside the club.

Some hours had passed since his lunch with his father and it was nice to have a chill, relaxed night to clear his head. He had met Indigo for dinner and then took her to Club Low to end the night with some dancing. She stood before him wearing a sleek sleeveless dress. She wore her hair in four Ghana braids and the makeup on her face was flawless. Even though he felt that she didn't need the extra help he would be lying if he said that she hadn't gotten a rise out of him. Especially with the way her ass sat up because of her heels. Drake's song "Back to Back" was playing loud and clear, and the two of them were at the bar getting more shots.

"Me too," David Jr. said. "And you looking good as hell, too."

"Thank you for the hundredth time." Indigo giggled and batted her long eyelashes at him.

David Jr. was happy that she had given him a second chance because it gave him a chance to redeem himself. He didn't want her to think he was a womanizer and he also wanted to get to know her mind better. At dinner the two found out they had more in common than they thought. Both had fathers who lived the fast life and both had grown up feeling distant from them. He found out that one day she hoped to open a hospital whose purpose was to help patients with mental illnesses. He felt himself falling deeper into her charm, especially when he got to know her heart.

"Ay, man! Your dad's club is always popping!"

Roland appeared at the bar with his date and gave his boy a handshake. When David Jr. told him that he was going out to the club that night he invited himself to tag along. He was always up for life in the fast lane.

"That nigga don't know how to do shit if it's small." David Jr. grinned and motioned for the bartender to pour two more shots.

"To . . . us!" Indigo put her shot glass in the air and turned to David Jr., who grinned down at her.

"To us!"

"Y'all corny. Let's just take this mothafuckin' shooooot!" Roland yelled and threw his back.

The rest of them followed suit and that added to David Jr.'s buzz greatly. Indigo pressed her body to his, and put his hands on her ass. Placing her lips by his ear she whispered, "I want to feel what Sheila felt." She leaned back so she could look lustfully up into his eyes. It was apparent that she was tipsy and that the alcohol was talking for her.

"You're drunk," David Jr. said but the alcohol was controlling his body. He squeezed her soft bottom and looked at her full lips. He wanted nothing more than to see what they were capable of.

"And horny," she said, licking her lips. "What, are you worried that I won't call you tomorrow?"

David Jr. laughed and looked at the ground before looking back into her face. "You sure you ready for all of that?"

"Take me somewhere so I can show you."

He grabbed her hand but before walking away he nodded his head at Roland, who gave him a knowing look in return.

"I see you, boy!" Roland grinned and then turned back to his own date so that he could talk her into giving him some play.

David Jr. led Indigo through and off of the crowded dance floor. "This way," he said, taking her toward the elevator. "Come on."

Once inside he hit the button to close the door and then another one to stop it so that it wouldn't go up. Indigo couldn't wait any longer because she pushed him against the wall and placed her lips on his. Her tongue swam freely in his mouth and intertwined with his while their hands explored each other's bodies. He placed his hand up her skirt and pulled her thong to the side, yearning to feel her wetness.

"Mmm, David Jr.," Indigo moaned loudly when she felt his thick finger slide inside of her.

Taking charge, he flipped her around so that it was her back that was on the wall, and he dropped to his knees. He wasn't sure if it was the alcohol or the fact that she made him feel things that no other woman had up until that point; whatever it was he wanted to use his tongue. He rarely ever licked pussy but for her he was making an exception. He put her right leg on his shoulder and lifted her skirt up. Before she could interject his tongue was giving her clit a lashing so good that she almost asked him what she did wrong.

"Right there! Yes!" She had never had anyone give her head so good and she gripped the back of his head so that she could fuck his face. "Uh! Uh! Davidddddd! Awwwhhhh!"

He made her reach her orgasm in under five minutes and she felt her walls clenching and unclenching. When he looked up at her and read her body language, he knew what she wanted.

"You want this dick?"

She nodded her head and bit her bottom lip. When he stood up she helped him unbutton his jeans and her eyes almost popped out of her head when she saw what he was working with. She stroked his shaft and used her thumb to massage the head.

"I'll go easy," David Jr. said, seeing her wide eyes. He put one arm around her and hoisted her up while using the other hand to position his dick to her opening. He thrust one time and had to bury his head in her neck. Her pussy was tight and felt like heaven. "You so wet, Indigo. Damn."

Placing both hands on her round ass he pushed her into him as he pushed into her. She wrapped her arms around his neck and let her screams fill the elevator. Their lips met again and the connection between them grew with each thrust until they both had reached their point of climax.

"I'm about to come! Ahhh! I'm about to come, David. Yessss, please don't stop!"

David Jr. felt her begin to shake violently in his arms, and felt the warm gushiness that escaped her and flowed onto his shaft. He couldn't hold his in any longer. He pulled out of her so that he could squirt on the wall behind her but what she did surprised him. She pulled away from him and dropped to her knees. Wrapping her lips around the head of his penis just when he started shooting, she pushed it to the back of her throat. He felt her throat working as she swallowed each drop of nut that escaped it.

"Fuck!" He threw his head back and placed a hand on his forehead as her head bobbed back and forth. "Damn, girl."

She stood up, wiping the corners of her mouth and grinning. "You drank me. I wanted to return the favor."

The mixture of alcohol and good sex took its toll on her because she stumbled back into the control key of the elevator. When they started to move David Jr. looked and saw that she had accidently hit the button that led to floor three. He buttoned his pants back up and helped Indigo fix her dress.

"Where are we going?" she asked nervously. "I didn't mean to hit anything."

"It's cool," David reassured her. "My dad's office is up here. I don't think he's there, though. I'll show it to you."

He pulled her to him and gave her another kiss. He heard the doors behind him open and when he turned around the smile and the bliss that he was feeling wiped away instantly. The entire hallway leading up to his father's office was splattered with blood.

"What the fuck?" David Jr. said and stepped cautiously off of the elevator. Indigo stepped off with him and the doors shut once again behind them.

"Da . . . David, what's going on?" She looked wide-eyed around the hallway and put her hand to her mouth. "Is this a joke?"

"Stay right here," David Jr. instructed and then walked slowly toward his father's office.

It was slightly open and he knew that was sign number two that something was wrong. His father never left the door to his office open, even if he was in it. When he got to the door he pushed it open with his hand and the smell hit him first. He used a finger to flick the light switch on. What he saw when the lights illuminated the room was enough to make all of the food he'd eaten that day come up instantly. He doubled over as he vomited and dropped to his knees. When he was able to catch his breath he began yelling.

"No! No! Fuck! Fuuuuccckkkk!"

Indigo decided then that it wasn't in her best interest to listen to what he had said about her staying where she was. She walked to where he was and put her hand to her nose when a stench so strong hit her. What she saw was something that would forever haunt her dreams. She looked inside of the office and gasped. Sitting in a chair staring directly at them was a body that had been beaten so badly that the head had been deformed. The pool of blood on the carpet under the chair was still wet and the body had been tied to the chair, forcing it to sit up. Whoever it was didn't have a shirt on anymore and there were two visible bullet wounds in the shoulders. On the brown chest there were letters carved there, three Ds, and the first one was crossed out.

"Who is that, David Jr.?"

David Jr. didn't answer her. With a shaky hand he reached inside of his pocket so that he could grab his phone and make a phone call. When he heard the familiar voice on the other end he took a breath before speaking.

"Day, it's Dad," David Jr. said into the phone. "He's dead. King David is dead."

Chapter 10

"All my shit better be in here, too," Day snarled at the young'un her dad had working his main trap. "Don't play with me."

"Count that shit then," the guy she'd come to know as Cane said to her.

"Ay, watch your mouth, little homie," said one of the goons Day had brought with her to collect.

They were all standing in the back of the house in what should have been the kitchen of the house. The wall separating it from the living room had been knocked down, turning it into one big room. Behind Cane were women in thongs, bras, and face masks, cutting and bagging product. Standing around them were three of Cane's big, bulky niggas making sure that they were really doing their job and not getting high off of the product. Cane stood there tall and slightly muscular. He had light yellow skin and tattoos that covered his arms. He was of Native American descent so his straight-back cornrows were long and went down his back.

"Nigga, shut the fuck up," Cane said, letting the goon know that he put no fear in his heart. "You ain't nobody."

Day rolled her eyes at Cane because every week it was the same thing. If David Jr. thought she couldn't stand him he hadn't seen how she reacted whenever Cane was around. Every other house that she collected from showed her respect just off GP, but Cane was a different story. He never flat-out hated on her, but he let it be known that just because she was the boss's daughter wasn't a reason for him to go out of his way for her.

"I don't ever have to count it any other time, do I?"

"Then what you asking for?" Cane asked her and looked at her like she was stupid. "You the one who is late, anyways. We were just about to close shop so you lucky you even caught me."

Day returned the look of disgust but to that she didn't have an answer. She was indeed late doing collections that day and he wasn't going to let her live it down. It was known that the main trap switched locations every day just to keep a low profile. Too much traffic went in and out of it for it to stay in one place. Cane stayed on top of his business and he was ruthless. These were reasons why King David had pulled him in from being a street runner and given him a real position to make money.

"I was up late bodying niggas so that we can all continue business," she snapped back. "So you're welcome."

"You said sorry wrong."

"Nigga, just shut the fuck up sometimes!" Day couldn't help the smile that came to her face and she turned away before he could see it. She made her way to the door with the duffle bag in tow. "Fuck you, Cane. I'll see you next week."

"Whatever." Cane waved his hand at her but his eyes automatically traveled down to the way her ass moved as she walked away. He couldn't front; li'l mama was probably the baddest chick he had ever laid eyes on. On an off day she was a ten, but her attitude dropped her down to a solid six.

"When you gon' try to get those?" he heard one of his homies, Tre, say from behind him.

Cane went back to the big, plush chair that faced the front door and he leaned back into it. From the side of it he picked up the AK-47 resting there and put it in his lap. "Never," he responded.

Outside, Day made her way to the all-black Lexus that she was riding in. Her driver held her door open and when they were both settled inside they pulled off with two more vehicles in tow behind them. She was just about to go home and get some more sleep. She had been putting in so much work for her father's empire that she barely had time for herself anymore. She was tired and she couldn't think of any better way to spend her alone time than in the bed, cuddled up in her blankets, eating Cookies 'n Cream ice cream.

She checked the time on her phone and saw that it read a little after two in the morning. Just as she was about to put her phone back into the pocket of her Levi jeans, her brother's face popped up on the screen. She had half a mind to ignore the call, but after what had happened in the basement of Big Mike's house she figured he might want to talk about it.

"Hello?"

"Day, it's Dad," she heard her brother's voice say. He sounded like he was in distress. "He's dead. King David is dead."

Her heart went cold and it was almost as if time around her had stopped. Day wanted him to take back those words and tell her that he was playing a joke on her. "Wh . . . what? What do you mean 'dead,' David Jr.?"

"He's dead, Day. I'm in his office. S . . . somebody killed him in here."

"You're at the club?"

"Yeah."

"Stay there. I'm on my way." She disconnected the call without saying goodbye. "Hey! You! Go to Club Low, now!"

They weren't too far from the club, but still it seemed as if it took a lifetime to get there. By the time they pulled up the club had let out and everyone was in the parking lot being loud and having fun. Day didn't wait for the car to stop all the way before she jumped out, and ran on the red carpet to the entrance doors and past the security guards. She pushed her tan Ugg boots and didn't stop until she got to the elevator. She knew her security couldn't be too far behind her but she couldn't wait for them; she had to get to her brother. She pressed the UP button until the doors finally opened and she did the same thing to the number three. As the doors shut she saw the black suits running, trying to reach her, not understanding what was wrong with her or what she was doing.

Ding!

She finally reached the third floor and burst out of the elevator. The smell hit of death hit her before her eyes traveled the walls of the hallway. She spun around as she walked and put her hand to her mouth while she took in the sight of all the blood. By the time she had done a complete 360 she was at the entrance to the office. The door was open, and it was never open. When she saw him she dropped to her knees at his feet and let out a bloodcurdling scream. He was strapped to a chair and it was apparent that he had been beaten to death. He had bullet wounds to his shoulders and gut and his once handsome face was so badly deformed that she couldn't even recognize him. The only way that she could tell it was King David was his socks. His favorite socks.

"Nooooo!! Ahhhhh! Ahhh! Daddy!" She banged her fists on the floor repeatedly as the sobs escaped her body. She wrapped her arms around her stomach and rocked forward and backward. "Noooo!"

She felt someone come and wrap his arms around her. "Get up, Day," she heard David Jr. say. "You're in his blood."

He helped his sister to her feet and put her head on his shoulder so that she wouldn't have to see the gruesome sight at hand. He had to close his own eyes because that was not how he wanted to remember his father. He looked in the corner and saw Indigo sitting in a chair, staring at her hands. Before he could say anything to her the office was swarmed with security. They all let out sounds of despair and disbelief when they saw what had happened to their boss.

"Prince David, Princess Day, follow me."

They were all ushered out of the room. David Jr. reached his hand back and grabbed on to Indigo's. That was the first time Day had taken notice of her. She eyed her but her heart was too shattered to speak. She didn't have any words to say.

"Get them home. Tell his wife what has happened. 'Round-the-clock security on the house. No one is to go in or come out for the next twenty-four hours!"

The head security guard, Mac, barked out orders; and for Day and David Jr. the two hours were a blur. David Jr. didn't even remember saying goodbye to Indigo when she was whisked off. The next thing he knew they were at his parents' house, sitting in the living room with his father's most trusted men. Their mother sat on the couch beside them, clenching her robe and looking much like a ghost. Her eyes accidently made contact with the bloodstains on the tips of Day's shoes and the knees of her jeans. She had to clench her eyes shut and look the other way.

"What has happened tonight has been tragic," Mac softly said from the couch on the opposite end of them. "It was unfortunate and nobody could have predicted something so awful to happen. We have men who will be working around the clock to find out who did this. When we find them we will make sure they get what they deserve."

Day, whose eyes were puffy and bloodshot, nodded her head, wanting whoever did her father like that to die the most painful death. Beside her, between her and David Jr., her mother shook her head violently.

"This was his own fault!" she said, allowing the tears to flow freely down her face. "Killing who did this won't help! Whoever did it is after my whole family and it is his fault! All that shit he did is finally starting to catch back up to him and he has killed all of us for it!"

"Ma—"

"No, David Jr., don't you see? We are all dead! I knew I should have packed you kids up and left a long time ago. Whoever did this wants all of us dead."

"Shut the fuck up!" Day screamed and jumped to her feet. She pointed her finger in her mother's face. "Don't nobody want your gold-digging ass! My daddy hasn't even been dead a whole twenty-four hours and you are already talking bad on him! I see why he never came home!"

David Jr. tried to calm her down but she pulled away from him and she snapped on him too. "Do you know what has just happened? Do you get it?"

"He was my dad too, Davita!"

"Since when? You never showed him love, no matter how much he busted his ass for you. But his death is the least of our worries now." She plopped back down on the couch and put her face in her hands.

"What do you mean?"

"A war," Mac said. "Somebody has just ignited a war."

David Jr., who was still consoling his mother, looked to where Mac was sitting. He then looked at the solemn faces of the men around him, and then to his sister. It seemed that they all understood something that he didn't. "What do you mean a war?"

"I don't think this is the right time to discuss this," Mac said and nodded toward Angela.

"Take her ass upstairs," Day said, sitting back up. "We need to discuss this. Now. I'm not going to be able to sleep tonight anyway."

One of the men stepped forward and grabbed Angela's arm gently and helped her stand to her feet. She gave no protest. She was exasperated and the only thing she wanted to do was lie down and forget everything that she had been told.

When she was gone Mac turned his attention back to the twins. "Did your father ever tell you how he came to be king of St. Louis?"

"Yeah."

"No."

David Jr. and Day both answered the question at the same time, and Day turned to her brother and turned her nose up at his lack of knowledge. "I guess I forgot that you spent all that time on your mama's titty."

"Not now, Day," Mac said. "Since you don't know, David Jr., I will tell you. Both King David and I started as simple dope boys. Making runs for the trappers in our neighborhood. At the time the king of St. Louis was this nigga named Cabo. He was real ruthless. Some might have even called him evil. Well, when he was murdered there was a war in the streets. Everyone was fighting each other."

"Why?"

"For his crown. He didn't have any children to pass the title to, so it was up for grabs."

"I thought that the crown went to whoever got his connect."

"Exactly. In this day and age the only way the best connect will fuck with you is if your name carries weight in the streets. And the connect wasn't fucking with nobody after Cabo died. Not until he met King David."

"How did my dad get his attention?"

Mac smiled at the memory. It was the day that King Davis had actually risked his life for him. "We were at the trap house that we ran for Cabo. We had the last of his product, about two hundred thousand dollars worth. Some niggas came up in there trying to get the dope, and started spraying and shit. But your dad? Nah, your dad wasn't no bitch. He picked up the AK and started spraying right back at them niggas. In the open, too. My nigga dropped at least six of 'em. But they just kept coming. So I stood up and started shooting too. I thought we were both about to die that night. But we just kept knocking 'em back and reloading until we were the last two in the house. Then I got hit." Mac lifted his shirt up and showed them a bullet wound on his torso. "He told me to hide behind the couch and that he wasn't gon' let them kill me. Long story short, your dad held his own against twenty niggas. In a small-ass trap house. He was the last man left standing."

David was intrigued at the story about his father that he never knew. It made him want to call him up and ask him to go to breakfast in the morning. The lump in the back of his throat stopped his thought process when realization hit him. He swallowed and focused back on Mac.

"Who were them niggas who ran up inside the spot then?"

"That's the kicker." Mac chuckled. "They were the shooters for the connect, coming to collect the rest of Cabo's unpaid debts to him. After that it was a wrap. I guess he liked how your father moved, because the next week the streets were calling him King David. Your father is a street legend, which makes the manner of his death so sickening. Whoever did this wanted him to feel it. The entire time."

Day's elbows were on her knees and she rubbed her hands together. Without looking up she asked, "So that's what you think is about to happen? The streets are about to go crazy?"

"It's what I know," Mac said solemnly. "King David was the only thing holding the community together. He finally had rival gangs being semi-peaceful toward each other; the whole city was eating. With him gone, there will be no glue."

Day nodded her head. "And what about us?"

"Ain't nobody gon' get y'all on my watch."

"How long can you keep this news under wraps?"

"The street is the biggest grapevine. But twenty-four hours. Tops."

"Who is the connect?" David Jr. asked the question that had been lingering in the air since Mac had finished telling the story.

Mac looked David Jr. directly in the eyes. "Nobody knows. He was going to tell you, but I guess he never got the chance."

David shook his head and took a deep breath. Day stood to her feet, not able to listen to anymore. "Looks like all those years of pushing Daddy away finally paid off. Now we're all dead."

"Day!" David Jr. called her and stood up when she stormed off to her room. "Day!" It was at that moment that he needed her the most. He had never felt so lost in his life. Just a week ago he had everything mapped out. It was crazy to him how fast things could come crashing down right in front of his face.

"Let her go," Mac said. "We have some things to discuss. The meeting on Saturday."

"Wh . . . what?"

"You have to go in your father's place. That's what he would have wanted."

"Mac, my dad just was murdered. I don't want to talk about that right now." Everything was happening too fast. He just wanted to take a timeout and think.

"I understand that, kid, and I'm sorry you're this old and still don't get it. In this life there are only two ways out: a sticky end or a good one. Either way life goes on around us and business does too. This is the biggest meeting for the

Mason name and it is imperative that someone with the Mason name is there. I know that you and your father were not close and I am sorry that it's me telling you this and not him. But before tonight your father was working on a very important deal. And my job now is to keep you alive until then."

"What kind of deal?"

Mac took a deep breath and told David Jr. something that King David had told only him. "He was planning to go legit."

Chapter 11

The homegoing service for King David had to be the biggest in St. Louis history. Even though it was a closed casket, the service was a beautiful one. The songs that played there actually brought tears to Day's eyes, and she never cried in public. Every street within a five-mile radius of the church had been closed. And the ride to the grave site was the saddest one of her life. She never expected to have to say her final good-byes to her father so soon.

She and David Jr. rode in the same limo but sat on opposite ends and stared out their own windows. Angela rode in her own separate car because she had to go to the house and prepare it for people to come and pay their respects to the family. They had barely said a word to each other since that night. At the site they waited for everyone to say their goodbyes before they got out to say theirs.

David Jr. walked ahead of Day so that he could say his first. His placed a hand on the casket. "There was a lot I didn't know about you. I guess that's my fault, huh? I'm sorry. I'll make this right. I promise."

He couldn't say anything else because of the lump in his throat. He blinked his tears away and motioned for Day to come forward. She replaced him and, too, put her hand on the white casket.

"Even in death you're a king, Daddy," Day whispered and let the warm tears stream down her face. A small sob escaped her lips. "It wasn't supposed to be like this. You supposed to still be here. I don't know how to do this without you. I love you, Daddy. Rest in peace."

She stepped back and nodded to the man in a black suit that it was okay to lower him into the grave. David Jr. stepped forward once again and the twins watched the casket drop six feet slowly. Once it reached the bottom, together they both dropped their white roses.

"I am so sorry for your loss."

"He is in a much better place."

"God has him in His arms now."

Angela, David Jr., and Day stood in the hallway of their family home receiving condolences and cheek kisses until Mac told them that the lawyer was there to read them King David's will. They excused themselves and allowed Mac to keep everybody busy while they were gone.

Although Angela was genuinely upset about her husband's death she knew it would happen sooner or later. She was just upset that when it happened her children's lives were threatened in the process. If David Jr. was murdered there would be no hope. She knew that King David had finally taken her advice and given David Jr. more of his assets, and she could finally coerce him into doing what she wanted to do with her husband's businesses. She wanted to sell them. All of them.

"Good afternoon, everyone, my name is Mr. Thomas Blake. I am here to read you David Anthony Mason's will," the lawyer started once everyone was seated in the family room. "I am very sorry to hear about your loss, and hopefully this will make it hurt a little less."

"Thank you," Angela said a little too eagerly and Day glanced quickly her way.

Mr. Blake was an older white man in his late forties with a white mustache and beard. He put his circular glasses on his face and removed a couple of pieces of paper from his briefcase. Day smiled because the light from the window allowed her to see the writing through the paper.

She wasn't able to make out what the words said but she would recognize her father's scribble anywhere. Before he started reading, Mr. Blake cleared his throat.

"'To my dear daughter, Davita Arial Mason, I leave my hair salon Blessings. She has always loved that place like a second home. I want her to expand it and to open up many more Blessings here and out of the state. I also leave her Club Low in hopes that she will keep it fun and classy as I have done all these years. I release all the money in my offshore accounts to her. She will see that they hold a little more than five million dollars. And, lastly to my dear daughter, I leave the house that she grew up in.'"

When the lawyer read the address Angela's mouth dropped open. "Bu . . . but that's this house. Why would he leave you this house?"

Mr. Blake ignored her and continued reading. "'To my son, I leave you . . . everything else.'"

The lawyer went on to list everything else that King David had owned, on top of the amount of money he was leaving him, and David Jr.'s eyes opened wide. He had no clue that his father owned so much, and the fact that he was now the owner of it all completely took him by surprise.

"What am I supposed to do with all that stuff?"

"Figure it out," Mr. Blake told him. "Because it is all yours now."

"Okay. Okay." Angela waved a hand to get Mr. Blake's attention. "What about me?"

"Oh, yes! You! How could I forget this? This is the most important part of the letter."

Angela smiled and leaned back in her seat, knowing that her husband must have gotten her a new house if he'd given this one to Day. She thought about how good she and Aman would look in a new bed together. She was tired of sneaking around with him after all those years.

"'To my wife, my cheating wife, I leave absolutely nothing.' Okay, well that concludes that! Any questions?"

Day almost choked on her tongue when she saw her mother's face. David Jr., on the other hand, was more interested in the content and what was actually said in the letter.

"Cheating? You were cheating, Ma?"

Angela paid him no mind. Instead she snatched the letter from Mr. Blake's hands and reread the words there. "It can't be," she whispered, and flipped the papers from front to back as if looking for more words. "When did he remove me?"

"Maybe this will explain some things," Mr. Blake said and handed her an envelope with her name on it. "Mr. Mason was always a sharp gentleman. That's not to say that he predicted his own death, but he knew the likeliness of it was very high.

In whatever case he told me it was extremely important that I give you this letter to read."

Angela snatched it from his hands and ripped it open. What she read made her drop to her knees and begin to cry.

Angela,
When did you stop loving me? I was everything that you ever wanted in a man, but I guess that wasn't enough for you. When it came to you I tried to keep the image of the girl I met on those school steps alive for so long that I guess I didn't see what you have really become: a woman with no soul. You care only about yourself. You wouldn't even put your own children before you. I know why you wanted me to releases my assets to David Jr. and I know now why you have kept him so close to you. You want to sell everything I own so that you may flourish off of it. What he chooses to do with what I have left him is his choice, not yours. Also, I found out about Aman a long time ago and I want you to know I am not angry. I am happy you found somebody to pass the time while I was always gone. So to you I leave you nothing

of my personal belongings; however, I do give you your freedom. You are free to live and do as you want without my money, my cars, or my home. Hopefully our son sees you for the monster you truly are.

   King David

"What does it say, Ma?" David Jr. asked, standing to his feet to read over her shoulder.

"Nothing," she said, walking to the door. "It says nothing."

"I'm sorry, Ma," David Jr. said. "I was going to try to talk him into putting you back in the will."

Angela whipped back around. "You mean you knew I wasn't in the will and you let me sit here like a damn fool?"

"I didn't think about it, Ma. I'm sorry."

She looked at her son like she didn't recognize him and he did the same to her. She threw her hands in the air and continued her path to the glass door that separated the family room from the rest of the house.

"I threw my whole entire life away for what? For nothing!" She opened the doors and shouted at all of the guests. "Get out! All of you! Just get the fuck out of my house!"

"My house," Day said and cleared her throat.

"Not now." David glared at her. "And you aren't kicking her out." He could already read her mind and that was something that he wasn't having. Whatever had gone down between his parents had been between them. At the end of the day she was still the woman who gave birth to them.

"I'm not," Day huffed and crossed her arms. "I'm not that fucked up. Go calm her down. The damn shit just started. Somebody needs to eat all the food."

David Jr. sighed and gave his thanks to Mr. Blake before he went off to find his mother. He was telling everybody that she was just going through it, and he got many sympathetic responses back. They told her that she had gone upstairs, and he was about to go follow him but something caught his eye. Somebody, to be exact. Indigo stood in the foyer of the home wearing a long black dress with a hat on her head. The hat had a veil on it that covered half of her face, but David Jr. would recognize her lips anywhere.

"I'm so sorry for your loss," she said when he walked up to her. Her hand found its way to his chest and rested on the cotton of the jacket to his suit. "I'm sorry I wasn't able to make it to the funeral."

"Stop saying sorry," David Jr. told her. "It's not your fault."

She gave him a sad smile. "Was that your mother who just ran out here yelling at everybody to get out?"

"Yeah, that was her. She's just going through a hard time right now."

"I bet. I was like, damn, I just got here! I haven't even gotten to see my boo yet."

"Your boo?" David Jr. raised his eyebrow at her. "When did I become that?"

"Right now," she said and stood in her flats on her tiptoes to plant a kiss on his lips. "Hopefully that took away some of your pain."

David Jr. smiled down at her and put a hand on hers.

"Who's this?" Day had finally exited the family room and she ran smack dab into David Jr. and a girl wearing an old lady hat. She was confused because she wasn't sure if she had ever met her before. "David Jr., who is she?"

"This is Indigo," David Jr. said. "Indigo, this is my twin sister, Davita."

"Wow," Indigo said and put her hand out. "That's crazy. You look just alike."

"We are twins, like he said. And nobody calls me Davita. You can call me Day," Day said and shook the girl's hand. When she got closer to her she remembered where she recognized her from. "Wait, you're the girl I saw the day . . . the day—"

"Yes," Indigo quickly jumped in so Day wouldn't have to say it. "That was me."

"I'm sorry you had to see that," Day said with sincerity in her voice. She then turned back to her brother and pointed to the kitchen. "I'm about to go make a plate before all the niggas eat everything. Then I'm going home. My head hurts from all this shit."

"We aren't supposed to leave," David Jr. informed her.

"Whatever." Davita rolled her eyes and made her way to the kitchen.

"She reminds me of your mom," Indigo tried to joke. She didn't like the solemn look he wore on his face.

"Yeah," David Jr. said. "That's because you never got to officially meet my dad."

The two walked through the house until they reached the patio door that lead to the huge backyard of the house. Indigo was instantly blown away. The whole yard was green and neatly trimmed. There was a hot tub, a fire pit, and a tall tree that had a tree house.

"Is that a real tree house?" Indigo asked when David Jr. opened the door.

"Yup." David Jr. smiled while looking at the big wooden house. "Day and I used to call it our getaway house. Whenever our parents would make us mad that's where we would go. We made our dad put two entrances on it and split it in half so we would have our own space."

He helped her step outside and the pair made their way a little ways away to a table in the shade. David Jr. pulled her chair out so she could sit down before taking a seat himself. She looked at him with wonder in her eyes.

"What?" he asked.

"It's just weird, that's all."

"What's weird?"

"That you guys are twins . . . and I get the vibe that you aren't very close at all."

"Because we aren't close. At all." David Jr. laughed. "We are twins."

"So you guys get your own birthdays at least," Indigo analyzed. "But still that's your sister, and especially after what has happened you should definitely use this time as bonding time. Can I ask a question, if you don't mind?"

"Shoot."

"What did you mean when you told her that you two aren't supposed to leave the house?"

David Jr. took his time answering. He didn't want to scare her off, but he figured if she was still there after what she had seen then she knew what was up. "Whoever killed my dad is still out there. And you saw what was on his chest. Three

Ds, and one of them was crossed out. That can only mean that Day and I are next. We can't really move the way we want to until the killer is caught."

"But what about school? This is your last year."

"I don't know," David Jr. said. He didn't need to mention that he had just become a millionaire and honestly didn't even need to go to school anymore. He sighed.

"So how will I see you? I gotta come over here."

"If you want to see me, I'll make time for you," David Jr. said. "If you don't mind being surrounded with at least twenty niggas."

She laughed and he was thankful she was there. She was keeping his mind off of the things that were really bothering him.

Chapter 12

Angela waited for everybody to leave to before she opened the door to her room again. She was heartbroken. Not only had she lost her husband, but in his death her dignity went as well. Everyone had always thought that she and David had the perfect love story, but they didn't know all the things she did to get to where she was at. Although she and David had met at a very young age the two didn't start dating until she was almost twenty-one, the same year he had become King David. After they met the first time Angela knew she liked him, but she just couldn't see herself dating someone like him. He was rough around the edges and not at all like the man she always envisioned for herself. Not only was he from the streets, but he was poor. Something she never told David was that her parents cut her off when she was eighteen, so she wanted a man with money.

After high school she went to college and found that it was much harder than the school in East St. Louis. She struggled with her classes and almost failed her freshman year. It wasn't until her sophomore year when a few of her professors were showing her the kind of attention a professor shouldn't show a student that she figured out just how much power she held. She was young, beautiful, and had a body that most girls her age wished they had. She began using it to get her what she wanted and when she wanted it.

Angela's first victims, of course, were her teachers. All of the classes she chose were with male professors. Some were married, but she didn't care. They got their nut and she got her grade, along with a few other material items. She preyed on her professors all the way until she graduated. Top of her class, at that. She didn't stop there. She took many powerful politicians and even some celebrities to her bed just to make sure she maintained the lifestyle that she had grown accustomed to living.

However, when she ran into David Mason again and saw how well he had flourished, she knew she had to have him and only him. For, if she got him she would only have to sleep with him and only him for the rest of her life. In a way she did love David, but she could honestly say that she loved his money more. At first, she put on a front and played the part of the girl he met in school. But after she got the ring she slowly but surely began to show her true colors. When she got pregnant she was even happier because no matter what happened she thought she would always have access to her husband's money.

She wanted the best for her children, but she wanted the best for herself more. Through all the love she gave them, she always loved herself more and would always put herself first. She tried to form a bond with Davita at an early age but it was apparent even then that she was a daddy's girl. David Jr., on the hand, always seemed moldable. She knew deep down that even though the two children were twins David would leave everything to his junior, and because of that she needed David Jr. to stay in her pocket forever.

As they grew, she poisoned Davita's head with lies about how a woman should be. Although she put up a front that the street life wasn't what she wanted for her children, she silently guided Davita toward it. She taught her daughter how to use men to get what she wanted, and she passed along her love of money. For David she wanted him to be a scholar, just like she was, and grad-

uate with a degree. Up until that moment everything had been going as planned. But in the end
it all had backfired on her.

She sat alone in her room wearing a silk robe
wrapped over her nightgown as she brushed her
hair in the mirror. She could still see the beauty
in her own face, but she had to get past the sadness first. She couldn't believe that, after all the
years she put in, she ended up with absolutely
nothing. The only thing that she had left was
David Jr.

"You okay, Ma?"

A voice surprised Angela. She looked in the
mirror of the vanity that she was sitting at and
smiled when she realized that she must have
thought him up.

"What's wrong, Mom?" David Jr. asked with
curiosity in his eyes.

"Today has just been a long day," Angela said
with a sigh and set the brush down.

"I know, for me too. I'm just trying to figure
out who would do Dad like this. The way they
did it, it was sick and twisted."

"You'd be surprised how many enemies your
father had, David Jr. He has been king for several
years now, and he's made several enemies who
want his head on a stick. I just never thought
that they would ever try to come for his family,

but I guess in situations like this there are no exceptions. In the life that your father lived it was inevitable that he would meet a sticky end. I just don't want that for you or your sister."

"You try telling Day that. She lives and breathes the life of hustling. She loves everything about it."

"I can't. You have to, because she won't listen to me, especially after finding out that I cheated on your father. She won't listen to me because she doesn't understand."

David Jr. didn't respond to that because that was something that he didn't understand. To his knowledge his father had been a lot of things, but the one thing he never heard of him doing was stepping out on his wife. Even though he had a strange way of showing it, family meant something to King David. David Jr. didn't want to think about their mother being with another man. The thought made him sick to his stomach.

"After they find the person who did this to your father you both have to leave this street shit behind you. You have something going for yourself, baby: you're about to get your degree. Day owns two businesses and is set for life now. What y'all need to run the street for? It's time to put that life in the casket with your father. It's time for a life with the fresh starts and new beginnings. He always wanted the best you; now all have to do is make a decision. These stories never end well, David Jr. Do you want to end up like your father, or do you want to live your life the way a real man is supposed to?"

David took a moment to think over her words. She was right; he definitely didn't want to die the way his father had. Whenever he thought about it a knot formed in his stomach and it felt like he couldn't breathe. That memory would plague his mind forever no matter how much he tried to remove it.

He leaned on his mother's vanity and looked down at her, hoping to get some more guidance. "What should I do, Ma?"

"Sell it. Sell everything. You may be a junior but that doesn't mean that's how you have to live your life forever."

The news of the death of King David had caused an uproar in the streets of East St. Louis. The streets had gone absolutely chaotic. It seemed as if nobody was safe unless they were locked away in their homes. The ones who had been dubbed the most loyal to King David had turned on him and started to rob his trap houses. With David Jr. and Davita shut away in the house for safekeeping there was nobody available to balance it all out. There was nobody to put fear in the hearts of the people, and there was no leverage between gangs. In three days the murder count went up to fifty bodies. Instead of thinking that maybe the chaos was due to absence of King David, the police department blamed it completely on him having power in the first place. In their eyes, if nobody like King David existed at all there would be no reason to act the way that these people were acting. They were acting like savage animals. There were more robberies and break-ins in history and not enough officers to take all the calls.

Detective Avery sat in his chair in his office, contemplating his next move. He was sad about King David's death, but not for the reason that most would assume. He was sad because a five-year investigation had come to a screeching halt without any retribution. He was sad that he hadn't been able to hit him with any criminal charges. There had been days where he dreamed about the look on King David's face when he put the cuffs on him and hauled him off to jail in the back of a police cruiser. He dreamed of the day when the judge sentenced him to life in prison. Now he would never get that satisfaction, so he had to settle for the next best thing.

"I need somebody to give me a warrant to search Davita Mason's apartment now. This case has dragged on way too long!"

Even though David Mason was dead, Detective Avery was still hell-bent on bringing down his whole operation. He knew that Davita Mason was a big part of his whole empire. He also knew that if anybody would take over everything then it would be her or her brother. He had done extensive research on David Jr. and found nothing to worry about. He learned that David Jr. despised his father and everything he did; he was just a college boy. So his main focus was on Davita. His main goal was to knock out the new queen before she was even crowned.

Ever since the mysterious disappearance of his star witness Antonio he had eyes watching her moves every day; still, however, she managed to stay ghost most of the time. He had gotten some new interesting news, though. Ever since the death of her father, he found out, she had been staying at the family house, for the past few days. Why she was there, he didn't know. He was just happy that she was out of the way and that her house was vacant. Now the only thing to do was get a search warrant and hopefully find some of Antonio's DNA in her home.

***

"Where you going?" Day's voice shocked David as he tried to tiptoe down the stairs.

He looked back and saw his sister sticking her head out of her bedroom. He was wearing a pair of navy blue Air Max Classics, a pair of 501 blue jeans, and a navy blue Polo zip-up hoodie with a red Polo insignia. He was trying to sneak out of the house and he was positive that nobody had heard him. After talking to his mother, he went to his room and saw that he had a few missed calls from Indigo. She told him that even though they had made plans for her to come over the next day, she really wanted to see him sooner than that. He told her that he would see if he could get out of the house.

"I'm going to mind my business, damn. And don't tell anybody that I'm gone. I'll be back soon."

"Nigga, I ain't no snitch. You going to see that girl, huh?"

"What does it matter?"

"Because inquiring minds want to know. If you want me to keep my mouth shut you don't have to be rude," she snapped, but then softened her tone. "And I've never seen you actually like somebody before. She must be a good one."

"Yeah, she is. I do really like her."

"Did you first night her?"

"Bye, Day," he responded, grinning. "I'll be back before they know I'm gone."

"You do know that they're at the front door, right? And the back and the sides? But if you go out my window and slide down the rail they won't see you."

David looked suspiciously at his sister, wondering why she was trying to help him. Still, she had a good point. He turned around and went back up the stairs toward her room. He couldn't remember the last time he had even been in there. Everything in there was new to him, even though it was clear that it was from back when they were kids.

"Is that a B2K poster on your wall?" he asked her, pointing to the boy R&B group. "I didn't even know you had their CD."

She felt her face get hot from embarrassment. She loved B2K when she was younger and now that she was older she refused to take down the poster. She put a hand on his back and pushed him to the window. "Shut up and just hurry up and get out of here before they come up here and catch you."

She pulled out a pistol and handed it to him. "Whoever killed Daddy is still out there and I just don't want them to catch you slipping. I ain't ya mama so I can't tell you what to do, so I'm just going to say be careful."

David Jr. grabbed the gun from her hands without speaking and went out the window. Indigo said she was parked around the corner so all David had to do was get there. He was tired of being cooped up in the house; and nobody had a lead on who had killed King David. The video tape from the security camera that night had gone mysteriously missing. It seemed as if there was no hope in finding his father's murderer; and even with that being said he didn't want to be stuck up in the house for years.

Mac kept stressing the fact that he needed to keep him alive until the meeting on Saturday, but that was a whole four days away. The only thing sitting in his room for days had done for him was make him feel more guilty about how he acted toward his father until the day that he died. He kept thinking back to when he last saw him at Ruth's Chris for lunch. He felt that maybe if he would've kept them out a little longer then he wouldn't have even gone to the office.

Whenever he turned on the TV all he saw was death in the city. King David had only been laid to rest a couple of days ago, and the city already went up in flames. Mac had been right. They were all fighting to be the next kingpin. Brothers were robbing each other. King David's operation had taken such a big loss that they had to shut down shop. Everybody was angry because nobody was eating. All David thought of was how he felt whenever he was with Indigo. At that point in life she was the only one who seemed to bring him peace.

He felt like a child all over again having to sneak out of his parents' house the way he did in high school. But he felt that she was worth the ridicule. When his feet touched the ground he took off running before anybody could see him. He reached the front of the house and saw two men standing patrol. He thought fast and grabbed a rock from the bush that he was hiding behind and threw it high in the air so that it would hit the part of the house that was behind them. When they left their post he grabbed a couple more rocks and hoped his decoy trick would work again at the gate. It did, and when the guards there left their posts he slid his muscular body through two of the bars with some difficulty. Once he was through he looked behind him to make sure nobody had seen him. He put the hood to his Polo hoodie over his head, and began in the direction of where he'd told Indigo to meet him.

He half walked, half ran down the street until saw headlights flickering. He knew it was Indigo because it was the signal he told her to give when she saw him. He put his hand in the air to let her know that it was him, and she pulled up next to him so that he could get in the car. He looked over to where she sat in the driver's seat, and smiled because she looked beautiful to him.

"Whaaatttt?" she asked when she noticed the way that he was looking at her.

"You just look good."

"Boy, I am in leggings and a T-shirt."

"You still look good." He leaned over and kissed her. "Thanks for coming through and getting me out of that house."

"You good; don't thank me. How are you holding up?"

David Jr. shrugged his shoulders, trying to find the words to explain how he felt as she did a U-turn in the middle of the street. "I mean, being stuck in the house I've been going crazy. And every time I turn on the news I see something else. Everybody is killing each other."

"How much longer do you have to stay put?"

"Until they find whoever killed my dad, or until this meeting on Saturday."

"What meeting on Saturday?" Indigo asked, keeping her eyes on the road.

"Before my dad died he told me about some big meeting that he and I were supposed to go to together. But now since he's gone I have to go by myself."

"Wow. Those are some pretty tough shoes to fill. How are you feeling about it?"

"Shit, to be honest I have no idea. I don't know what to expect. Everybody expects me to be exactly like my father. But I'm not him. You know? It's only been three days since he died and I haven't even had the time to really mourn."

"I understand. When my father died it was the hardest thing that I've ever had to deal with. He was the glue that kept my family together. So when he was gone he took a piece of my family with him."

"Well, this is one thing that I wish we didn't have in common. But we don't have to talk about all that," David Jr. said, changing the subject. "Where you taking me?"

"Just this old spot that I like to kick it at. It's where my dad took me when I turned twenty-one and got me my first drink."

"Where is it at? In the hood?"

"Kinda. Why, you scared?" Indigo smirked at him.

"I ain't never scared. I just like to be aware of my surroundings. I am King David's son, after all." It was the first time that he'd ever said that phrase with pride.

They made small talk the rest of the ride to the bar that Indigo was talking about. It was in a small white rinky-dink building across the street from a family-owned convenience store. There were drunken old heads hanging outside, talking smack to each other and laughing. The streetlights lit up the whole parking lot where she found a space.

"Don't worry; it's nothing but old heads in here. Ain't nobody going to bother us. Come on." Indigo got out of the car and waited for David to follow suit. When he did he walked around the car and grabbed her hand so that they could walk side by side.

"Aw, sookie sookie now, look at the lovebirds coming through!" an old man with missing teeth said. "You looking good, sugah. If that young man ain't doing you right you coming back out here and see me. You hear?"

"I guess you'll never see her again then, old man, huh?" David Jr. said, laughing.

When David got closer the old man squinted his eyes. "You look mighty familiar, boy. What's your name?"

"Uh." David contemplated not telling the old man who he was. But when he sized him up he didn't think he could do any harm. "My name is David Jr."

"As in David Mason Jr.?"

"Yeah, that would be me."

"Well, I'll be damned." The old man stood up and shook David Jr.'s hand. "Your daddy is a legend in these here parts. Grew up right down the street. Look, I'm sorry to hear about what happened to him. That ain't right."

David Junior didn't want to really get into the details much. So he thanked the man and excused himself to go inside the bar with Indigo.

"Look at you, you a celebrity or something?" Indigo joked.

"No. My pops was the celebrity, not me."

Scoping the bar, David Jr. could tell that it was a spot that an older crowd hung at. There were dartboards on the wall, two pool tables, a jukebox, and a square bar was in the middle of the joint. Indigo pulled him to two empty barstools and got the waitress's attention.

"Excuse me, ma'am. Can I please get a liquid cocaine?"

When she reached in her purse to grab her debit card David Jr. stopped her, and pulled out a crisp twenty dollar bill from his pocket and handed it to the bartender. "When you're with me don't you ever try to pay for anything."

Indigo looked at him with flirtatious eyes and gave him a small smile. "Okay. You're the boss. 'I get it, I get it. Your hustle don't ever go unnoticed, baby. I'm with you. I'm with it.'"

David Jr. couldn't help bursting out with laughter as she referenced the Drake verse. "You think you're smooth."

"I can show you smooth." She leaned in and sucked on his bottom lip. "Mmm, you taste so good."

David Jr. took in the woman before him. She wasn't wearing any makeup and her hair was pulled back in a simple ponytail. She looked tired, but that didn't take away from her natural beauty. He was beginning to really feel her. He knew a long time ago that she wasn't like the other girls.

They talked for a little while longer over shots, and when they both were feeling a buzz they decided to take over the dance floor. He pulled her in close as they danced to the sound of Usher's voice crooning through the speakers. It was the first time in a long time that he'd enjoyed a woman's company without being intimate at all. There was something about the way she smiled up at him and the way her eyes looked like they were holding something back. He didn't mind, though; he planned on learning everything about the girl in his arms.

"What are you thinking about?" Indigo whispered in his ear.

"Nothing, just about how I want you to be around for a while."

Indigo was taken aback for a second but then she caught herself. She cleared her throat and hugged him tighter to hide the shock on her face. "Really?" she whispered.

"Really."

Before the two got to say another word to each other, the door of the bar burst open and a group of young thugs entered all toting weapons.

"Ay! Some old head outside this bar just told me that King David son was in here. So where you at, nigga?"

David Jr. looked around the bar and saw the older couples ducking under their tables. The sight of the weapons terrified them, especially with all the death plaguing the area. He pushed Indigo behind him and stood his ground. "I'm King David's son. What's good?"

"You got a price on your head, boy, and I've come to collect."

"A price on my head? And who set this price?" he asked, thinking that maybe it was whoever had murdered his father.

"Everybody out here in these streets, nigga. Everybody out here tryin'a be the next kingpin. I figure if I kill you then that makes me that nigga, right?"

"I don't think it works like that," David Jr. said, trying to buy himself some time.

The young'un in front of him shrugged his shoulders. "Shit, it's worth a shot." He pointed his gun at David Jr.'s head and began to apply pressure to the trigger.

"If you kill him I kill all of you niggas."

A familiar voice boomed from the entrance of the bar and startled all of them. David Jr. looked behind the young'un and saw Mac standing there with five more goons, all holding automatic weapons.

"Get the fuck out of here and don't let me see your face again, little nigga, or I'ma blow it off. "

"A'ight, man!" The boy waved his hand at his friends and they ran through the clearing that the goons had made for them.

Mac's murderous stare was on David Jr. He glared at the stupid young man before him and he wanted to slap him. The only thing that saved him was the fact that he was the son of his best friend. "What were you thinking? Nigga, didn't I tell you how dangerous it is out here for you? Hurry up and get in the car."

"I'm not a kid, Mac."

"You sneaking out the house like one. Tell your girl bye and let's get out of here. I don't know how many more people know you're here." Before Mac left he looked at the girl David Jr. was with. There was something familiar about her face but he couldn't put his finger on it. "Do I know you?"

She shook her head no but didn't speak. He stared at her for another moment before turning and walking out of the bar. David and Indigo followed soon after and he hugged her after walking her to her car.

"I'ma text you," he said. "You still coming by tomorrow?"

"Shit, if they let me through the gate."

David Jr. grinned down at her and shut her door. "They will."

Turning his back on her he walked and got into the black Audi that Mac was in as well. They sat in the back seat in silence for half of the ride because both of them had bad attitudes at the moment.

"How did you find me?" David Jr. finally broke the silence.

"Both you and your sister have trackers on your phones. Your father's orders."

Even from the grave his father still looked after them. David Jr. suddenly remembered what his father had said to him the last time he saw him: *"There is no place on this earth that you can go and not be King David's son. Understand that."*

"Thanks," David Jr. said, looking at the his shoes.

Mac didn't respond and David Jr. understood. He put his hands in his pockets and leaned back in his seat. "I didn't ask for this."

"You didn't have to."

"Why?"

"Because it's yours."

Chapter 13

Ever since it had come to light that Angela was having an affair Day had steered clear of her. The house was big enough that the two of them didn't have to see each other if they didn't want to. Day's loyalty would always be to her father and she couldn't believe that her mother would step out on him. After everything that he'd done and sacrificed to give her the life that she wanted. When she was a teenager her mother would always tell her that women had the most power in the universe. It was apparent that she was a firm believer in using what you had to get what you wanted. It never dawned on Day that her mother would be bold enough to sleep around. She was happy that her dad didn't leave her mother anything, because she didn't deserve it. She had done a good job at avoiding her so far but soon her luck ran out.

Day was in her room rummaging through an old photo album. She shut herself away that day, not wanting to be bothered by anybody. David Jr. was somewhere downstairs with the girl named Indigo and she just wasn't in the mood to be bothered with anybody else. The last couple of days had been very hard for her but she didn't tell anybody about the pain that she was feeling; she didn't want to talk about it. The more she talked about it the more real it became. Everything had happened so suddenly and she hadn't had time to wrap her brain around it. She had been crying herself to sleep every night and no matter how much she tried to push the tragedy to the far back of her mind, it always came back.

She still couldn't believe that she would never see her father alive again. She didn't want to believe that she would never see him smile and hear him tell her how proud of her he was. She didn't want to believe that it had really been him tied to the chair. There was so much more that she wished she had the chance to say to him, and now she would never get that chance. The hardest thing for her to cope with was the fact that she wasn't able to say good-bye. Out of all the things that King David schooled her on, the one lesson he forgot was how to go on without a father.

As she sifted through the photo album she passed many pictures of David Jr. and her when they were kids. She stopped flipping pages when one specific picture caught her eye. She, David Jr., and their dad were flying a kite at the park. She smiled, remembering that it was taken on her fifth birthday, and she was so happy. Even though she and her brother were twins she loved the fact that they didn't have to share a birthday. On her day her dad would do whatever she wanted to do and on David Jr.'s he was able to do what he wanted. That year all Day wanted was to have a picnic in the park by the water, feed the ducks, and fly a kite. To that day it was her favorite birthday party. Looking at her brother's face she could tell that it was one of the happy times; their smiles said it all. That was back when they were a whole family. Now they were just two fucked-up twins with a ho for a mother.

Knock! Knock!

Day looked up to see who had come to interrupt her thoughts. When she saw who it was knocking on the door she wanted to kick herself for even thinking about her mom because she felt like she must have thought her up. Angela pushed the door open slightly. She stood there wearing a pink Gucci jogging suit with white Nikes on the feet. Her hair hung loosely around her pretty face and she looked at Day as if she hadn't thought about what she was going to say yet.

"Hey," Day said.

"Hey, Davita," Angela said softly. "I know you must not like me very much right now."

"I can't disagree."

"Aren't you going to let me explain my side of the story?"

"What do you mean, your side of the story? You were a married woman. There shouldn't be any 'your side of the story.'" Day felt her anger surge and she slammed the photo book closed. She got up from the bed and walked toward her bedroom door. "Excuse me," she said and slid past her mother.

Angela grabbed her arm softly to stop her but Day snatched away. Being that close to her, Day could smell the alcohol on her breath. She shook her head, knowing that Angela was either tipsy or drunk out of her damn mind.

"No. I'm not tryin'a talk to you right now. You're foul. I just can't wait for all this shit to be over so I can go back to my normal life."

"That's what you don't understand, Davita," Angela said, following her down the stairs and into the kitchen. "Our lives will never go back to normal. Your father is dead, which means all of this"—she waved her hands around in a circle—"is yours and David Jr.'s. I am very sad at the loss of your father, and I did love him, whether or not you believe me; but maybe it happened for a reason. I agree with you, baby. It is time to leave all the shit behind us. It is time that we put an end to the cycle. All you and David Jr. have to do is sell everything and start fresh. Your dad wanted the best for you."

Day stopped filling her glass with water so that she could turn around and look at her mother like she was a fly on the wall. She couldn't believe the words coming out of her mouth. But looking at her face, Day could tell that she was dead serious.

"So what's best for me will be for me to sell what my dad left to me?" She scoffed. "You are so sad, do you know that? That's not what he wanted and you know it. You know what? I think that you're just mad that he didn't leave you anything, so you don't even want us to have it. You're mad because you can't go run off with that nigga. That's it, isn't it?"

"No, it's not," Angela said even though she felt her face going red. "I've already talked to David Jr. about it. He's giving it some serious thought. He wants to leave all this dirty money behind. He never wanted anything to do with your father's business dealings and I don't understand why you do. You are a young, bright, beautiful woman. Why do you want to patrol the streets like a man? You can still go to scho—"

That's where Day had to cut her off. "I should have known that you and Mr. Perfect teamed up on this one," Day snapped with fire in her eyes. She was pissed off that she had helped David Jr. the night before and he was going behind her back and discussing things with their money-hungry mother. "I can't talk to you right now. I just can't do it and I just need for you to leave me alone. Daddy didn't give you any money so now you're trying to get it out of us. You are one sad bit—"

"Watch your mouth! I am still your mother!"

"Barely!" Day looked Angela up and down with a look of disgust on her face. "Everybody knows that David Jr. was always your favorite. You pushed him to do the best but encouraged me to be a ho like you! But you want to sit up here and act like there is something wrong with the lifestyle I live! Yes, you are my mother, and I am grateful to you for bringing me into this world, but starting right now I'm not fucking with you. Now go powwow with your golden child and get the fuck out of my face, Angela."

It was obvious that Day had finally reached her breaking point. Sh e turned her back on

Angela and grabbed the glass that she had just filled. She took a gulp and hoped that it would calm her nerves. Angela stood there and looked at Day like she was the spawn of the devil. Day's words sliced through her like a sharpened knife. Seeing that approaching her in the first place had been a bad idea, Angela turned her nose up at Day's back and sneered.

"Fine. You want to be like your father so badly?" she spat. "You'll end up just like him. Dead."

She left Day where she was standing and stomped back up the stairs to her room. When she got there her eyes brushed over the empty bottle of wine that had been knocked over on her vanity. Any other time she would have hurried to set it upright, not wanting anything to drip on the floor, but right then that was the least of her worries.

She and King David had separate walk-in closets, each on an opposite side of the room. Deep in hers, hidden behind a wall of shoes, was a duffle bag that she had packed a long time ago just in case she ever got the courage to leave King David and go be with Aman. There weren't any clothes in the bag; instead, there was $200,000. The liquor in her system was controlling her thoughts and actions, but she had made the decision to leave and not come back. There was nothing left for her there and after talking to Aman the night before it was clear that he still wanted to be with her. It was time for her to move on with her life. Davita and David Jr. would have to fend for themselves.

Slinging the duffle bag over her shoulder she went back downstairs and into the kitchen to where the key holder hung on the wall. From it she snatched the first set of keys she could find, then made her way back out of the kitchen.

"I'm leaving."

Day's eyes went to the duffle bag on Angela's shoulder and she already knew where her mother was going. "Humph. Daddy hasn't even been dead a week and you're already hopping into bed with another man."

"I was hopping in bed when that man was still alive," Angela threw over her shoulder, and power-walked to the front door.

"I'm sorry, ma'am. I can't let you leave," one of the black suits keeping watch at the front door said, and held his hand up to stop her from going any farther.

Angela hit his hand away from her and kept walking toward the door. She opened it and dared anyone else to try to stop her. "Bite me! Whoever killed my dumb-ass husband wants them. Not me!"

Angela left them all standing there and went to the roundabout driveway in front of the house. With all the family cars there she wasn't sure which keys she had grabbed, so she pressed the button on the remote. When the doors to Day's black Camaro unlocked she hopped inside of it and threw her bag in the back seat.

"Hey! That's my car!" Day yelled coming out of the house to stop her mother from stealing her vehicle.

"Buy a new one!" Angela shouted before shutting the door. "You have the money."

Day was running down the stairs in front of the house so Angela hurried up and put the key in the ignition. The last sight she saw was her daughter hitting the last step and running toward the car with her hand reached out. As soon as she turned the key over the whole car blew up. Day was knocked back from the force of the explosion. She landed hard on her back and, only a few feet away from her head, so did the hood of her car. Her ears were ringing and she tried to focus her eyes but the only thing she saw was smoke. She heard somebody calling her name but it sounded far away and she couldn't move her body. She began coughing uncontrollably with one hand clutching her stomach.

"Day! Day!" she heard David Jr. yelling over her. He reached down and scooped her into his strong arms and carried her to a spot on the lawn where the air was clear. He looked back at all of the security guards and shouted instructions to them. "Somebody go get me some water!"

The path to Day's lungs was cleared almost instantly. She coughed a couple more times, gasping for air. Her hand clenched David Jr.'s wrist tightly and he brushed the hair from her forehead. Indigo, who had been there visiting David Jr., showed up at his side with a glass of water.

"Drink this. Chill, it's okay," he said and helped her sit up. He saw that it was her car that had blown up. It was smoking and in flames. "What happened?"

"Sh . . . she . . ." Day burst into a fit of coughs and pointed to the car. She had to take another swig of water before she was able to continue. "She's still in there. Mom is still in there."

David Jr.'s body reacted before his mind did. He left Day with Indigo and he ran to where the burning car was. The explosion had been so powerful that it severely damaged the two cars by it; and the closer he got he could see a body still in the driver's seat.

"Help!" he shouted when he realized that he couldn't get close to the car to even try to get her out. "Help! My mom is in that car!"

From the house four of the security guards brought out fire extinguishers and started going to work on the car. Once they cleared the front of the car and David Jr. got to it, what he saw made his stomach churn. His mother was still in the car, but her skin had melted off of her face, her hair was completely burned away, and her head nodded forward. She had no life in her body but David Jr. didn't want to believe it. He tried to yank the door open with his hands but burned his palm.

"Fuck!" he shouted out. "I need this door open. Somebody open this damn door!"

He already knew that it was too late to save her, but still he wanted to try. She couldn't be dead, she just couldn't be.

"It's too late, son," Mac said, coming up from behind him and touching his arm gently. "She's gone. Come on, we gotta get you and your sister out of here."

David Jr. jerked away and began to throw wild punches in the air, yelling out in agony. The pain he felt in his heart was so excruciating he had to drop down to his knees, much like Day did when she saw King David dead.

"Come on, we have to go," Mac said and grabbed David Jr. by the arm again, that time with a firmer grip so that he wouldn't be able to pull away. He started shouting instructions to his men. "Powell, get Davita and go put her in a car so we can get them out of here. It isn't safe anymore. Harris, get Indigo and take her home right now. Turner! I need you to get me all the video footage from today and back all the way for a week."

Before Harris could grab her, Indigo ran to where David Jr. had just gotten back to his feet. She could still feel the heat from the car even though all the fire was out, and when she looked inside of the car she saw a sight so horrific that she had to turn her head. She looked into David Jr.'s eyes and saw that there were tears welling there.

"I don't want to leave you," she said and gripped on to his shirt and buried her head in his chest. "I'm not leaving you."

"She's coming with me wherever I go," he told Mac.

Mac was completely against that but he could tell that it was something that David Jr. would fight for, and they didn't have time for a debate. "Whatever. We just need to hurry up and get you and your sister out of here. Whoever put the bomb in your sister's car might still be around somewhere."

David Jr. and Indigo were ushered out of the house and led to a car that Day was already in. She looked better, just a little shaken up. When she saw David Jr. enter the truck, his face it confirmed it all.

"So we're orphans then?"

David Jr. didn't respond; instead, he just put his elbows on his knees and looked at the floor. Day nodded her head and swallowed the lump in the back of her throat. Indigo, who sat between them, reached for and squeezed her hand in empathy, and surprisingly Day squeezed it back. The three of them were driven to Mac's gated four-bedroom Victorian home, which had been deemed the next safest place on earth for them. Once there, Mac piled them all in the basement of his large house. He made his men stand guard upstairs while he talked to the twins. The girls sat on the couch, with Indigo trying to calm Day's nerves, and he poured himself and David Jr. shots of whiskey at the bar he'd had built.

"Take this. It will help numb the pain," Mac said and handed him the shot glass.

David Jr. didn't need to be told twice. He downed the shot and then grabbed the whole bottle from Mac and poured another. He wanted to erase the image of seeing his mother's burnt body. He could still see and hear the sound of her body sizzling inside of the vehicle. Mac took the bottle from him after he'd poured himself two more shots, and he instructed him to go take a seat by Day on the leather couch. Mac rubbed his chin hair and it seemed that wrinkles had formed in his once smooth golden brown skin. He contemplated where he should start and how he should say it. He figured that there was no other way to say it than to be blunt.

"Your mother wasn't a victim of a faulty vehicle. She was the victim of a car bomb."

"But I thought that me and David Jr. were the only targets," Day said.

"Exactly." Mac and Day locked eyes. "It was in your car, Day. That bomb was meant for you."

Realization set in, and Day understood that it was supposed to be her in the car and not her mother. The thought that she had come that close to death made her stomach turn.

"Did they see anything from the tapes?"

Mac shook his head. "Your mother must have turned off all of the security cameras, because the last time they were used was months ago."

"And you have no idea who's doing this? Or why?" David Jr.'s deep voice was relatively low.

"We are doing everything in our power to keep you two safe, but right now we don't have any leads on who is after you. We just know they want you dead for whatever reason."

"So we're just sitting ducks then?" Day looked at Mac as if he had just told her the most out-landish thing in the world. "How do we know it's not somebody in your camp? How could somebody put a car bomb in my car when it hasn't even moved for days? How do we know it isn't you?"

Her words came as an insult to Mac and he let her know it. "Don't you ever in your life let any stupid-ass shit like that come from your mouth when referring to me, understand? I would have laid my life down on the line for your father! I don't have to do any of this shit for either of you."

"Then why are you doing it?" David Jr. chimed in.

"Because I see the bigger picture, the picture that your father was painting, and it is my job to protect his children until the masterpiece is complete. I know that what you two are feeling is pain beyond the imagination but, Day, you should know firsthand what comes with living this lifestyle. Death follows death. It's just part of the game. I just need to make sure you both make it to see Saturday alive and then maybe we won't have to worry about any of this shit."

Mac wanted to add in there that he wasn't too sorry about the death of their mother but he knew that it was too soon. Yet, that still didn't take away from the fact that he had never really liked Angela. He'd always told King David that something wasn't right about her. He always got the vibe that if King David wasn't who he was then she wouldn't have even given him the time of day. Mac also had called King David crazy the day that he told him that Angela was having an affair and he never spoke a word of it to her.

"Okay," Day said, nodding her head. "I understand. But I'm not doing any more of this being cooped up in the house shit. I'm going home tomorrow. So that I can lie in my own bed. And I don't want any of your goons to come with me. I don't trust them niggas."

David Jr. nodded his head in agreement. "Yeah, Mac," David Jr. said. "I know that you're just tryin' to protect us but I'm not with the shit. I'm going back to my own crib."

"I'm going too, so he won't be alone," Indigo chimed in.

"And you can have your niggas stand watch there, but I'm not staying here." When Mac opened his mouth to object Day held up her hand and shook her head. "That's the deal or there is no deal. We already tried shit your way; now look. Another body was caught, and it could have been me. And I'm cool on your security. I have my own person in mind."

"Who?"

"Don't worry about that. Just know he's the only nigga out here as thoroughbred as me. If somebody wants me dead they gon' have to go to war to catch this body. You want me to hide up in this crib with you and a nigga who turned his back on his roots. I'm cool. I'll take my chances with a real street nigga."

David Jr. looked side-eyed at his sister and let the liquor do the talking for him. "Nigga, our moms just got killed and you sitting here talking shit? You just always sound so fuckin' stupid. Who you gon' shoot at? A ghost?"

"Fuck that shit that you're talking, David Jr. This shit ain't gon' stop until either we boss up and go after the mothafucka ourselves or we run. And I ain't no bitch. It could have been me in that car. Whoever is doin' this shit almost touched me."

"All the more reason to stay put," Mac interjected.

"Would my daddy stay put?" Day asked, and when Mac had no answer Day stood up and marched toward the stairs of the basement. "Exactly. I'm gone. Tell me when the funeral is."

On her way out, she snatched the bottle of whiskey that Mac and David Jr. had just taken shots from and took it up the stairs with her.

"I'll go after her," Indigo offered and kissed David Jr. on the cheek. "She's just upset, that's all. We all are."

Indigo bounded up the stairs after Day and found her in the living room of Mac's house alone, drinking straight from the bottle. She was shocked to see tears streaming down the side of Day's face. From the few times that she had met Day, Indigo definitely didn't think that she was capable of crying.

"Hey, hey," Indigo said, sitting down next to her and trying to grab the bottle from her hand. "Easy with that, girl. You're going to be drunk as hell if you drink all that on an empty stomach."

Day glared at her and snatched her arm away. "And who the fuck are you? You ain't my mama. Shit, both my parents are dead!" She threw back another swig and relished the burning sensation as it made its way down her throat.

Indigo sat there watching Day for a few more moments, and then she reached for the bottle again. "Well, since I'm here I might as well take a shot too," she said, and when Day looked mistrustfully at her she offered up a kind smile. "I come in peace. Shit, I never expected to date the son of a kingpin who got murdered. And I damn sure didn't expect to witness his mother get blown up in a car bomb." When she realized the way her words sounded, she cringed and said, "That sounded awful. I'm sorry."

"You're good," Day said and handed her the bottle. "Drink up. None of this is your fault. I'm just sorry you're in the crossfire."

The two sat in silence drinking the liquor until it was all the way gone. Day's tears had dried up and she was looking into the large fireplace in Mac's living room. The way the flames broke off from each other explained the way she felt inside: hot and broken.

"I caught my first body when I was seventeen," she whispered, catching Indigo by surprise. She was drunk and she didn't care who heard her confession. It was a story that she never told anybody. "It was after my senior prom. My date was getting a little too friendly with this girl I considered my best friend at the time, so I just left. David Jr. was there with his friends and he didn't even know I had left. He wouldn't have cared anyways. We may be twins but we have never been friends. Anyways, I was walking alone on this dark street. I don't know where I thought I was going. But this group of boys started messing with me. Trying to lift up my skirt and see what kind of panties I had on. One of them pushed me to the ground and started touching me between my legs. They were going to rape me. If I wouldn't have re-membered the razor that I kept in my clutch then they would have. I slit his throat right before he was able to penetrate me. His homeboys freaked out, I guess, because they all ran when they saw all the blood."

Indigo stared at the side of Day's pretty face. She could tell that she was clenching her teeth, because her jaw line was tense. The pain that Day had been trying so hard to hide the last few days read all over her face at that moment. The dried-up tearstains had created white streaks down the sides of her face. "What happened after that?" she asked when Day didn't continue.

"I went home and I told my daddy. I told him that I thought I killed somebody and he sent a car to where I told him the body was. After that he taught me how to defend myself and how to shoot a gun. Things that he wanted to teach David Jr., but he had to show me instead because his son wanted nothing to do with that part of his life. They both loved David Jr. more. They would never admit it. But they did, especially my mother. I was only as close to my father as I was because David Jr. wouldn't give him the time of day."

"I don't believe that. I think they loved you both equally."

"Well, I do." Day laughed spitefully. "And you never really knew my mother. She was a ho. Whenever I got a bad grade in school she would tell me to seduce my teachers and turn their frown upside down." Day shook her head. "That's some ho shit. I did it, though. She was my mom. I didn't think she would tell me to do anything that would end up hurting me. I had to work ten times as hard to earn my daddy's love, and all David Jr. had to do was ignore him. This meeting that they were supposed to go to, it should have been me he chose to go with him. Not David Jr. That nigga is scared to shoot a gun. It took him twenty-two years to catch his first body, but me? Me? I've been putting in work for the family business since I graduated high school. Before he died I actually saved him from catching a fed case."

"Wh . . . what do you mean?" Indigo sounded like she was afraid to know what she was talking about. The more she listened to her talk, the more she wondered if Day had a heart. The way she spoke of death and about killing people was almost unheard of.

Day laughed again and lay back on the couch. The cool feel of the leather on her neck soothed her and she closed her eyes. Indigo balled up on the couch and laid her head down as well. "This detective named . . ." Day slurred and giggled some more. "His name was Detective Avery Dickhead."

Indigo felt the alcohol take its effect and she began to giggle too.

"He arrested me and told me that I killed somebody named Antonio."

"Why would he accuse you of doing that?"

"Because Antonio was a fucking snitchhhh," Day slurred and dragged out the last word. "He was going to tell on my daddy and fuck up shit for all of us."

"So what did you do?"

"What I had to. No body, no case," Day stated and smiled widely.

"Day?"

"Hmm?"

"I think you're crazy."

"I am," Day said and let herself nod off to sleep.

Chapter 14

Business hadn't been the same since the death of King David. Everybody in the streets was hungry because the well had dried up. A couple of niggas tried to set up shop around town, but they always got either robbed or killed before they could really get up and running. There was no loyalty; everybody was turning on each other. There was no leader to balance out the chaos and there was nobody to put them in check.

Cane sat in his white BMW coupe that was parked on the side of the street with the door wide open. His left leg was casually out of the car with his foot touching the ground as he counted a wad of cash that was in his lap. He had just collected a debt from a man named Eric, who had just walked into the convenience store called Daily's. The two had agreed to meet in the little run-down neighborhood so that Cane could get the rest of the money from fronting him some work awhile back. Instead of pulling off, Cane sat there counting the money to make sure that it was all there and accounted for.

Ever since he had personally found out about the murder of King David he shut down his trap house and began to make his own solo moves. Cane always work best alone but when he met King David he knew that it was time for a change. He had never been hands-on in the business, but seeing the way King David moved made him want to be more proactive in the game. He was perfect for it, too. He was bred by the most thoroughbred of men and if a nigga bled the way he did then he figured there was no point in fearing him. He had just counted $2,000 when he heard a scuffle of feet running up to his car.

"Thanks for counting my money, dog. Now run that shit my way!"

Cane looked up and saw that he was looking into the barrel of a small handgun. He couldn't say that he was surprised; that was the third time somebody had tried to rob him in the last week. Instead of handing over the money, Cane leaned back and eyed the kid up and down. He couldn't have been more than eighteen. He wore dirty, baggy jeans and a shirt that had a hole at the collar. The Jordans that he wore on his feet were ragged and looked like they would fall apart any second. The look he had in his eyes was one that Cane had seen too often; the kid was hungry for a lick. He needed the money. Still, he didn't have the look of a coldblooded killer. Cane's eyes went to the hand that held the gun, and he could see that it was shaking slightly. Cane could tell by just looking at the kid that, even if pushed, he wouldn't pull the trigger.

"What's good, little nigga?" Cane asked. "You shouldn't point those things at people if you ain't gon' bust."

"Who said I ain't gon' bust? I'll blow your fuckin' head off, nigga. Now shut the fuck up and give me the money. Hurry up. I ain't got all day!"

Cane eyed the gun again and smirked. "Let me school you on some shit, young'un. Rule number one of the streets," Cane said, and reached for his waist. "Always remember to take your hammer off safety."

Cane had his own gun pointed at the kid in seconds. He put the money in his pocket so that he could cock it back and stand up from the vehicle. The boy was shaken up. He put his hands in the air when he felt the cold steel press to his forehead, and he wanted nothing more than to run in the opposite direction. His plan had completely backfired. Not only was the gun on safety, but he only had one bullet in the chamber. Truth was he had never shot anybody a day in his life. He'd found the gun in his father's drawer one night that he was passed out drunk. He was tired of living like a poor man so he decided that he would go out and hit a couple licks, thinking that he would finally get enough money to get out on his own. He was just hoping to scare the man in the car enough to get the money he'd seen him counting. That's all he wanted. Not to be standing on the sidewalk being punked out for the world to see.

"I could blow ya fuckin' brains out right here and now. Do you know that?" Cane asked, keeping the gun aimed up and at the boy's face. "What's your name?"

"My name is Tyler."

"Why you out here tryin'a rob people, Tyler?"

There were a couple of people who had stopped to watch what was going on before them. As long as they weren't the police Cane didn't care. It wouldn't be the first time that he committed a murder in broad daylight.

"The same reason you in that car counting money. I'm just tryin'a eat, man," Tyler said and held his head high.

Cane examined him for a few more moments before reaching with his free hand and snatching the gun from Tyler's hands. He looked down at the small Ruger and laughed. "This is a bitch's gun. What you doin' with this shit, kid?"

"It was my mom's," Tyler told him. "She died last year from cancer. I gotta do what I gotta do. It still shoot."

"Yeah, you're right about that," Cane said, looking at the gun one more time. He applied a little pressure to the trigger of his own pistol, about to make the kid's head snap back, but then he thought better of it. "You just gotta remember it's niggas like me out in these streets. You a guppy to us. I really should kill your stupid ass, but I don't think that will satisfy me. Plus, I got a way for you to earn this money." He lowered his weapon and leaned his back against the car.

He saw the confusion wash over Tyler's face when he realized that Cane wasn't going to kill him. "Word? What I gotta do?"

Cane checked the Ruger and saw that it had only one bullet in it, but that was all Tyler would need for what he was about to do. Cane nodded his head toward Daily's. "It's a nigga in there who just paid me this money back," Cane said, patting his pocket. "I fronted the little nigga some shit awhile ago, but now it seems to me that he is tryin'a play me. It was supposed to be four bands, but I have only counted two. I want the rest of my money."

"You want me to go bring him out here for you?" Tyler said, and figured that would be easy enough.

"Nah," Cane told him, shaking his head. "I want you to handle the whole situation. You got one bullet, my nigga. Make it count. Either he pay the rest of the money or he gets laid out. The only thing is that if you bust you need to make sure that you do damage. Niggas like him always run in packs. If he go back and snitch you out, you'll be dead before the day is over."

"What if I say no?"

"Then you're not as hungry as I thought," Cane said, and slightly shook the hand that his own gun was in. "And you'll still be dead before the day is over."

Tyler knew that he had truly picked his poison by running up to the flashy car with a gun with only one bullet in it. Cane handed him his firearm back and he looked to his far right at the convenience store. Outside of the building were fruit stands and a couple of bums begging for change. He squinted his small brown eyes and ran a hand over the waves on his head.

"What he look like?"

Cane gave him a full description, including what Eric was wearing that day. Tyler nodded his head and backed away from Cane. "A'ight," he said. He put his thoughts on the $2,000 that he would get if he handled that little problem. Then he stopped thinking that the man was just going to play him and drive off. When he turned his head he saw the man still leaning on his car and watching Tyler walk toward the store.

"I'ma be right here. When you handle that, come back."

Cane looked up to the convenience store and saw the sliding doors open. Eric walked out with a small paper sack and a smile on his face. He was laughing and yelling out something over his shoulder before the sliding doors closed behind him. Cane nodded toward Tyler and got back in his car without saying another word. He saw Tyler put the gun on his waist and jog toward where Eric was walking. Eric must have parked behind the building because that's where he disappeared to, and soon Tyler followed.

Cane honestly didn't think that Tyler would be able to hold his own against a nigga like Eric. Eric was a real-life street nigga, and when King David died he figured all of his debts to those who worked for him did too. Some let him slide, and some he had caught slipping. Not Cane though; he knew as soon as he pulled up to meet him that Eric was on funny time. The nigga had wrapped twenty one-hundred-dollar bills around twenty one-dollar bills. Cane didn't know why he didn't count it while he was right there in his face, but that was the reason he didn't pull off when he saw Eric go into the store. Because if something was off about the count he would just hop out and handle him right then and there. Tyler was just serving as the decoy and hopefully the little bullet that he had would wound Eric enough so that he couldn't run.

After about five minutes, Tyler still hadn't returned and Cane decided to go check things out. He got out of his car, placed his gun on his waist, and hit the lock button on his car key before he casually started walking in the direction of Daily's. He knew there was a small parking lot by an alley back there where crackheads liked to duck away and get high. He was just about to hit the corner of the store to get behind it when he heard the sound of a couple of gunshots go off. He pulled his gun out instinctively and put his back on the brick wall of the building. He heard one more shot sound and a cry of pain invade the air. He knew that the person shooting like that wasn't Tyler, because he only had one bullet. Pointing his gun, Cane took a step in the open, preparing to pull the trigger and blast anybody who seemed like a threat. What he saw shocked him.

"Well, I'll be damned, little nigga," Cane said when he saw Eric writhing around on the ground in pain from the bullet that Tyler had just put in his stomach.

Tyler had still been standing over him with his gun pointed to his face so that he could go through his pockets. From them he pulled out a big wad of money and he felt his eyes grow big. When he heard Cane's voice he looked up at him and held the money up. "This what you wanted?"

"Hell, yeah," Cane said, walking to where Tyler had Eric laid out on the ground next to his red Mercedes.

Eric was coughing up blood when he looked up and saw Cane standing there. His gun had fallen from his hand when Tyler had caught him slipping and he tried to make a weak grab for it. Cane saw what he was doing and kicked the gun underneath the car.

"Fuck is you doing, Cane?" Eric asked with bloodstained teeth. "This how you conduct business now? People pay you what they owe and then you kill and rob them?"

"You still owed," Cane said, kneeling down by him on the cracked concrete. Eric's blood had begun to stain it, but Cane knew that many men's blood had been spilled in the back of Daily's. "You still owe me two bands."

"Man," Eric breathed, clutching his stomach and trying to sit up on his elbow. "You know I'm good for it. I was gon' get you your money, dog."

"That's the second time you lied to my face," Cane said, looking at the reflection of the sun in his weapon. "How much money is that in your hand, Tyler?"

"Like, five Gs."

When Tyler answered, Cane turned his attention back to Eric. "You got five racks in your pocket and you couldn't pay me back my money when you had it?" Cane chuckled. "Say sorry."

"Fo . . . for what?" Eric asked, turning his nose up.

"For picking such a stupid reason to die." Cane stood to his feet and aimed for Eric's head. He fired his gun twice and made Eric's head bounce on the concrete.

Tyler's face was expressionless as he watched the blood pour from the back of Eric's head. He shook his head, knowing that Eric had truly fucked up in the game. He bit the hand that fed him. Tyler tried to hand Cane the money, but Cane shook his head and put his gun back on his waist.

"That's yours, kid," Cane said. "Keep that shit. For a job well done. Come on."

The two men ran back around the opposite side of the convenience store and back to where Cane's car was parked. It was obvious that everyone in eyesight had heard the gunshots go off, but nobody had gone to see what had happened. Cane was positive as soon as he and Tyler were gone they would all go back and view Eric's dead body. Somebody would probably steal his car and the fancy designer shoes on his feet; that's just how the game went.

"Did you physically touch him?" Cane asked.

"No."

"Is that gun registered?"

"No."

"Good." Cane reached in his pocket and grabbed the $2,000 from it. "Here. This is yours, too."

Tyler shook his head and declined the money. "You came back there and handled the rest. That's your money. I already got enough." He motioned to the bulge in his pocket from the money he'd taken from Eric.

"That money was your bonus. This is the real payment." He held the money out one more time and that time Tyler accepted it. "I got a question, though."

"Wassup?"

"You only had once bullet. The fuck was you gon' do standing over that nigga with an empty gun?"

Both men started laughing. Tyler shrugged his shoulders. "Shit, I guess we will never know." He put his hand up to give Cane a handshake. "Thanks, man."

It was an interesting plot twist but Cane shook the kid's hand. He looked at Tyler and saw a lot of himself in him. He remembered being a street rat and doing anything for a quick buck. "You need a ride, my nigga?"

"Nah, I'm straight," Tyler told him, shrugging. "I might as well just walk back to the crib. I don't get no ride any other day."

"Nah, that's not what I mean," Cane said and tossed his car keys to Tyler. "Here. I got another one just like it at the crib. The next time I see you this bitch better be shining."

Tyler didn't have another chance to say anything else to Cane because he began to walk in the other direction. He was confused about how his day had turned out. He had left the house with nothing but an old gun; now he was $7,000 richer and the new owner of a BMW coupe. He smiled, knowing that running into Cane had to have been his mom looking down on him. He gladly got into the car and saw that half of a blunt was waiting for him in the ashtray. He grinned, putting the key in the ignition; and he looked down at his clothes. He already knew where his first stop would be.

Cane looked back when he was a little ways down the street and he saw Tyler pulling off from the curb. It dawned on him that moment that he left his weed in the car, and he smiled, shaking his head. The little nigga had come across a gold mine when he tried to rob him.

Cane put his hands in the pockets of his cargo shorts and put his red Chuck Taylors to work. He could pull his phone out to call somebody for a ride, but a part of him wanted to walk and clear his head. There had been a lot on his mind, especially when it came to his thoughts about East St. Louis. In twenty years it was the second time that they had to close up shop around the whole city. That time he was sure nobody would rise up the way King David had. He looked around as he walked and was saddened by the sights. Since he'd moved to St. Louis from Louisiana when he was eighteen he didn't remember a time when the streets were so unsafe and dirty. He thought that maybe it was time to shut down shop once and for all in the city, set his sights on a new place, and per—

Hooonnnk!

The sound of a horn blaring interrupted his thought process. He didn't stop walking but he looked over his shoulder from where he was on the sidewalk. He saw a black Tahoe slowing to a stop in the street next to him. The windows on the vehicle were so dark that he couldn't see who was inside. His hand went to his waist just in case he had to pop off. Slowly the back window rolled down and, when he saw who it was, he removed his hand.

"Did I just see you give your car away?" Day asked, raising her perfectly arched eyebrow.

"Just doing my good deed for the day." Cane shrugged his shoulders.

"Get in," she instructed, opening the door for him and sliding over so that he would have room to sit. "Please," she added when he hesitated.

"I didn't even know that word was in ya vocabulary," Cane said to her and obliged.

When he got in, the driver pulled off as soon as he shut the door. He studied Day and saw that something was completely off about her. She wore sunglasses to cover her eyes, and the aura she was giving off wasn't that off the attitude-prone person he'd come to know. There was something soft about her. Her hair was in a disheveled bun at the top of her head, and she wore a light yellow Juicy Coutour jogging outfit. He was taken aback when he saw that she was wearing house slippers and no socks on her feet.

"How you been holdin' up?"

She opened her palms and shut them before she answered him. The last thing she wanted to do was let him see her vulnerable, so she cleared her throat before she spoke. "Somebody killed my mom."

"When?" Cane asked with an even voice.

"Yesterday."

"How?"

"There was a car bomb in my car and when she turned the key it exploded. She didn't make it out."

"Damn." Cane shook his head. "Hold up, did you say it was in your car?"

"Yup." Day looked up from her hands to look at him through her sunglasses. "It was supposed to be meant for me. My dad's security has been trying to figure out who's trying to kill us, but they haven't been able to yet. They don't want to get the feds involved because they don't want their noses sniffing in places that they shouldn't be."

"I feel that." Cane nodded his head. "So what are you gon' do?"

"I know whoever it is isn't going to stop until David Jr. and I are dead. Mac wants us to stay cooped up in his house until Saturday or until they find the crazy mothafucka. That's why I been out here looking for you."

"Why is that?" Cane asked. She was looking at him and he couldn't see her eyes. That bothered him, so he reached and removed her Dior sunglasses. When he saw how bloodshot and puffy her eyes were he understood why she had the glasses on in the first place. Without thinking he stroked her right cheek with his fingers. "Day."

"I can't be cooped up in the house with nobody, unless it's you," Day said seriously. "What if I would have been the one to get in that car? I don't trust nobody else to protect me."

Cane had half of a mind to tell her that he couldn't do it, but looking into her eyes he couldn't bring himself to say the words. She was in distress, and out of everybody in the world she could have called upon she had chosen him.

"Okay," he said. "A'ight, you can stay at my crib until all this shit gets situated. You got a bag or we need to stop at the store and get you some shit?"

Chapter 15

Detective Avery paced back and forth, running his hand from the top of his head all the way down to his chin. The last few days his office had become his room and his desk chair had become his bed. After getting the warrant to search Davita Mason's apartment he had gotten a little hope that he would find at least something to bring her in once again. He was wrong. When they kicked in the door or Davita's condo it was as clean as a freshly bathed baby's bottom. There was no sign of struggle or foul play, so just like that he was back at square one.

He inhaled deeply and plopped down at his desk. On top of it were files that covered the last five years. He grabbed one of the folders and an old photo fell from it. It was a picture of King David before he had risen to the top. The picture was a mug shot from when he was arrested for a petty corner store robbery. It was a day that Detective Avery would regret for the rest of his life. If he had done things differently back then, he wouldn't be in the predicament he was in now, and there never would have been a King David.

"We have a two-one-one in progress on State Street. Requesting officer backup immediately!"

"Ten-four," a young Officer Avery said into his receiver after listening to what the dispatcher had said. He was new to the force and had been picking up every job that he could in hopes to get in good with the chief.

His partner sat in the passenger seat of the police cruiser, and looked over at Officer Avery with irritation written all over his face as he drove. "Boy, you must love this job, don't you?" Officer Dobbs asked, referring to the fact that it would be the eighth call that they had answered that day.

"When I joined the force I swore to protect and to serve. We all did. I'm just doing my job, Dobbs. Do you have an objection to that?"

"No, I don't, and I understand that you want to do your job, but we only have fifteen minutes left. My wife made my favorite for dinner tonight and I'm just trying to get there. Are you sure you want to go? There are at least a dozen officers on patrol right now. It's probably just another one of those crackhead niggers trying to get a quick buck anyways."

The fact that he had used the word "nigger" so freely made Officer Avery feel a certain kind of way, and his emotions read on his face. Officer Dobbs saw that he had struck a nerve and almost took his use of the word back. However, when he thought better of it he didn't, because he meant it.

He didn't care that Officer Avery was a black man. To him the only thing that separated Avery from the rest of them was the uniform on his body. When he first learned that his new partner was a black man he had charged into the police chief's office angrier than all get-out. He was refusing to work with anyone the same color as the filth that he wanted to clear off of the streets. He requested a new partner immediately but his request was denied, so he had no choice but to work with the black man. Over the past few months he came to learn that Avery was one of the bearable ones, and they got along for the most part. Still, though, Officer Avery knew that Officer Dobbs was prejudiced just by the things he said.

Avery let the comment fly, not wanting to let it get the best of him. He had a job to do. He knew the moment that he signed up to be a police officer what he would be up against. Including him, there were only ten black offi-

cers on the police force. They had to deal with racial slurs and remarks all day and act like it didn't bother them. When they were out on the streets in uniform, the word "sellout" came out of almost every black man's mouth he passed. But just like the petty corner boys, he was just doing what he had to do to get a check.

Officer Avery had a hard childhood. His mother was addicted to drugs and his father would come in and out of the home. It was more peaceful when he was gone, because when he was home his alcohol problem caused him to beat on anything with a heartbeat. Officer Avery decided to become a police officer right after he turned twenty-one because he wanted to make a difference in the world. At the time, though, he didn't know how hard that would be; because at the end of the day it was still a white man's world. Black people just existed in it. Officer Avery tried not to let it all affect his way of thinking. He had a plan and that plan was to work his way up the totem pole so that his weekly checks would turn to salary, and so that he could buy the house of his dreams.

"The address is past the police precinct. If you want, I can drop you off to your car before I head over there. I understand how important dinner is these days."

Officer Dobbs gave him the side-eye before leaning back in his seat and taking a deep breath. He ran his fingers through his ginger-colored hair and shook his head. "No. I'll come for backup. Lord knows with those monkeys have with them."

For the second time that night Officer Avery brushed his words off like dust on his shoulders; and he turned the siren on. He did a U-turn at a set of lights to go toward the direction of the address that the dispatcher had given him. It took about five minutes to reach the destination and they hadn't even come to a complete stop when they heard the gunshots ringing out.

"Cover me. I'm going in," Officer Avery said, withdrawing his gun from the holster and jumping out of the car.

He didn't wait to see if Officer Dobbs had followed him; he just ran toward the shot-out glass door of the small store and mentally prepared for combat. He kicked the door open and got low to the ground as he walked. Debris was blowing wildly around in the air and all but one of the lights in the whole store had gotten shot out. His eyes instantly went to the dead cashier leaning over the front counter. Blood was leaking from his head and forming a small circle of blood on the ground below him.

He looked around and saw an elderly woman holding a small child as she hid behind the chips aisle. When she saw the officer she used a shaky finger and pointed toward the front of the store. He nodded to her and mouthed the words, "It will be okay." He then pressed the button on the walkie-talkie that was on his chest so that he could request backup. He had heard multiple gunshots from the outside. He wasn't sure how many people there were armed and dangerous.

"There is a two-one-one in progress. I'm requesting backup immediately. Shots fired. I repeat, multiple shots have been fired!"

He held his gun up by his face and took a few steps to the front of the store. A couple more shots went off, and when he got to the front of the store he pointed his gun toward where he heard the shots coming from. There he saw a man wearing camouflage khakis and a black hood holding a woman by her hair with a gun pressed to her temple.

"Freeze. Police!" Officer Avery shouted out. He stood to his feet and revealed himself while aiming his gun in the man's direction. "Let the girl go and lower your weapon now!"

Seeing the police officer before him instantly caused the young man's entire body to surge with fear. His name was Pete Willis and he had

planned to just get in and out of the store a cou-
ple hundred dollars richer. He was only nine-
teen but the hard life he lived made him look
about ten years older than what he actually
was. The bags under his eyes confirmed that
he hadn't been to sleep in days, and the furrow
on his brow showed how angry at the world he
was. He was broke and hungry. The only way
he knew to survive was to rob others. His par-
ents had given up on him a long time ago and
put him out on the streets when he was only
thirteen.

  Pete looked around the store frantically. Avery
thought he was looking for a way out.

  "There is no way out of here," Officer Avery
said. "This place is about to be surrounded with
officers in a matter of seconds. Just give me the
girl and drop your weapon and nobody gets
hurt."

  Pete knew the chances of him getting out of
there alive were slim to none. And even if he
did he would never see the outside world again.
The officer was mistaken when he assumed that
he was looking for a way out; that wasn't it at
all.

  Pete's eyes immediately brushed over the
tiled floor that was smeared with blood from
the cashier. The man didn't want to cooperate,

*and he had made a sudden movement so he had
to blow his brains out. He lay slumped over the
countertop with the back of his head missing,
being as he'd gotten shot at such a close range.
He told everyone in the store that he would kill
them all if they didn't stay out of his way. After
that, he shot an elderly man in the chest to send
a solid message. That was when everything
went downhill.*

*Out of nowhere somebody in the store began
to fire wild shots at him. He didn't know who
it was so he started to shoot his gun blindly
around the store, causing everybody inside to
scream and take cover from the stray bullets.
His bullets knocked out the glass to the door and
all the lights in the place except one. Looking
into the eyes of the police officer he knew then
what the cashier had made a sudden movement
to do. He contemplated his next move and almost put his gun down, but then thought better
of it. "Why would I do that? So you can kill me?"*

*"I promise I'm not going to kill you, son. I just
want to see the rest of these people go home
to their families. Don't you want to see your
family again?"*

*"I don't got no fucking family. The gutter
raised me." Pete threw the girl to the side and
raised his gun to fire at the officer.*

Bang! Bang!

The young man had moved so quickly that Officer Avery didn't have a chance to react. He heard the gunshots and prepared himself for the pain to follow. When he felt nothing he used his free hand to feel all over his chest. When his fingers touched no blood or any open wounds he looked up to see that the young boy was lying dead in a pool of his own blood. Standing over him was another young man around his age holding a smoking gun loosely in his right hand. The boy was tall and slightly muscular. The clothes on his body were worn and he looked like he could use a haircut and a nice lineup. Officer Avery quickly recovered from the shock of the near-death experience that almost just taken place. Behind him he heard the door open, and Officer Dobbs ran in behind him with his gun pointed at the boy with the smoking gun.

"Put the fucking gun down, boy! Put your hands behind your head and drop to your knees slowly," Officer Dobbs shouted.

The boy looked at the officers and slowly did what he was asked. The woman who was just thrown to the side saw more officers coming in and swarming around the boy. She shook her head, trying to help. "No! No! It wasn't him. He was trying to help us!" she tried to explain, trying to get their hands off of him. "Please, no, you don't understand. It was him on the floor who did this!"

"Shut up and get out of my way!" Officer Dobbs said, pushing her to the side to get to the boy. He roughly handled him while he put the cuffs on his hands. "You have the right to remain silent. . . ."

Officer Avery was still standing there in shock when the woman ran to him. "You have to help him. David is a good kid. He was just trying to help us. Pete killed the cashier and old man Jenkins! David was just trying to get us all out of here alive!" She was herded out of the store by two officers, but she gripped on to Officer Avery's sleeve before they completely removed her. "These white mothafuckas don't care about us! To them all they see is a nigga with a gun. Help him, please. His mother just died. A case is the last thing he needs!"

Officer Avery pulled his sleeve from her and took a step back so that she could be removed from the murder scene. The place had already started to reek with death but he paid no mind to that; the only thing he was thinking of were the words of the woman. He knew she was right. And if it hadn't been for the kid then he would have been dead due to his own slow reflexes.

That night David Mason was booked, where he stayed in jail for a whole week before they finally released him. He wasn't charged and the fact that he had an unregistered weapon was swept under the rug, on account of a police officer's word that he had acted in self-defense.

Detective Avery threw the mug shot to the side and wanted to punch himself. If only he hadn't let that woman guilt trip him that night then he wouldn't be in the predicament that he was in now. He would have been able to save the streets of St. Louis before King David's reign even began.

With a heavy heart, he piled up all of the folders and started to put them in a box that he would take to where the rest of the boxes for unsolved cases went. Normally he wasn't a quitter, but he felt that he had wasted too much time and energy on a case that had no other leads. He would just have to wait until Davita was caught slipping, just like her father had been.

Suddenly, there was a knock at his door, and he was confused since he had been certain that he was the only one still in the office that night. He walked to the door and opened it.

"Yes?" he asked, but soon saw that he was talking to nobody but dead air. In the distance he saw the janitor mopping the floor, but nobody else was present. He whipped his head left and then right. "Is anybody there?"

When he got no answer he slowly backed into his office and shut the door. On his way back to his desk he felt his foot step on something on the ground. Looking down, he saw that it was a manila envelope with the words YOU'RE WELCOME written in red ink on it. Slowly he bent down to pick it up. Somebody must have slid it under his door.

He walked back to his desk and sat down, curious to see the contents of what was inside. He ripped the top open and turned the folder over to dump out the contents. The only thing that fell out of it was a piece of paper with an address written on it and the words:

Bring the dogs with you.

He picked up the small piece of paper and wondered what it meant. Leaning back in his seat, he tapped his mouth with his finger and debated what his next move would be.

"This is a nice place that you have," Day said, stepping into Cane's apartment.

They had spent the rest of the day together, shopping and getting Day everything she would need until she could finally go home. The two talked about everything that had transpired over the last week and all Cane wanted to do was take her mind off of it. He thought it was beyond fucked up that she had lost both of her parents so close to each other, but he would be lying if he said he had never seen it happen before. He had seen whole families slaughtered when it came to the drug business, and sometimes he was the one on the other end of the gun. Still, it did something to him to see somebody as put together as Day shed a tear. He didn't like it, so all day he did little things to bring the smile back to her face. He knew that he wouldn't be able to relieve all of her pain, but if he could ease it just a little bit that was good enough for him.

Cane stayed in the downtown part of St. Louis, and his three-bedroom apartment was at the top of a tall building that overlooked the whole city. He set down the bags of hers that he was carrying, and he walked her to where she would be staying. The room that he was letting her sleep in was smaller than the ones she had at home and in her parents' house, but still it was spacious. The décor was black and tan with an African theme about it. The pillowcases had pictures of lions on them and the handles on all of the furniture were animal paws.

"You been to Africa?" Day joked, setting her Louis Vuitton bag on the queen-sized bed.

"A couple of times, actually," Cane told her in all seriousness. "Can't be pro black if you don't know where you come from, you feel me?"

"You're half black, though," Day teased, and winked his way.

"Yeah, whatever. Get comfortable. I'm about to take a shower. You hungry?"

"Hell, yeah! What are you going to order?" Day asked, taking some clothes out so she could hop in the shower as well.

Cane looked at her like she was crazy. He held up his palms, and she looked at them, confused. "What I look like, ordering food when these hands make better food than half of the restaurants in town?"

"Now this I have to see." Day laughed and then faked a serious face. "Wait, no. You're supposed to be protecting me. You're trying to get me killed already!"

"Ha-ha," Cane said, pulling his shirt over his head. "You won't be saying that when you're coming in your panties because the food is so good."

Day's eyes traveled over Cane's exposed upper body. He was cut to be a skinny guy and the tattoos that covered his arms and chest looked like they were trying to tell her a story that she would love to read. She cleared her throat and tried to get the lust out of her eyes, but it was too late. Cane saw it, but he didn't dwell on it. He knew that she was in a vulnerable state, and the last thing he wanted to do was take advantage of King David's daughter in a time of need.

"Just knock on my door if you need me in the meantime," he said, and gave her body a once-over. "And I've been meaning to tell you all day that you wrong as fuck for them shoes. Ashy-ass feet."

Day looked down at her slippers and smiled sheepishly. "It was a long day, okay? Plus, David Jr. almost didn't let me leave Mac's. I didn't have time to grab shit!"

"Speaking of which, give shorty a call and let him know that you're straight."

With that he left her alone to unpack her things and unwind her mind. She almost ignored his suggestion but then thought better of it. After all, she and her brother were all they had left. She picked up her phone and dialed his number.

"Davita," he answered, and she rolled her eyes. He must have still been upset about what she said the night before.

"Am I interrupting your grieving?" Day said sarcastically.

"I don't think I'll ever stop grieving," he said, and the sadness in his voice made her check herself.

"Look, David Jr., I'm sorry for what I said about Ma," she said. "I wasn't as close to her as you were, but if you're feeling the way I felt when we found Daddy, I know you hurting. I ain't call you to get on your neck or nothing. I was just calling to say that I'm okay."

"Where are you at?"

Day slipped off her slippers and walked through the door of her room. She went down the hall toward where she had heard the shower turn on; and the softness of the carpet massaged her toes. "Safe," she said in a low voice, not wanting to get caught peeking.

"Okay. I'm still here at Mac's. They think they have a lead on whose been doing this."

"Good! Then we can go home and figure all this shit out. I called Jes earlier and she said the shop hasn't been the same. The manager at Club Low said that business has dwindled since Daddy's body was found. Nobody feels safe."

"Yeah, it's all bad. If I miss any more of my classes I'm going to lose my scholarship."

"Nigga, you have enough money now to send one hundred kids to school," Day reminded him. "Where is Indigo?"

"She needed to go home. I had one of Mac's men drive her. Hey, Day?"

"What's up, David Jr.?"

"How much do you trust Mac? I mean, you didn't even want to stay here. You think it was him? He was the only other person besides us who knew about Dad's office. And there was no way anybody could have gotten into the house to put a bomb in your car."

"I don't know," Day said, thinking about her brother's words. He was on to something. "I don't think Mac would cross Daddy like that. Plus, he's the one who's been watching our backs this whole time. I don't think he would do anything like this."

"A'ight, man. All of this shit is just crazy to me. What are you about to do?"

"Just eat dinner and go to sleep. You?"

"I think I'm about to go to Mac's gun range and shoot around for a li'l bit. Day?"

"Yes, David Jr.?"

He paused, and for a second she thought that he was about to tell her that he loved her, something that she hadn't heard him say since they were ten. And even then it was forced.

"Be careful," he finally said.

"You too." Day disconnected the call right before she pushed open the door to Cane's bedroom.

She didn't know why she was in there; she was just being nosey. His room was huge and it had high ceilings. He had the curtain to his window pulled back and his view of the city was beautiful. The night sky stared back at her, daring her to count all of the stars there. And the way the city lit up made her feel a happy feeling inside.

She tossed the phone on his king-sized bed and stepped gracefully over to the window, passing the entertainment system in front of Cane's bed. Placing a palm on the cold glass she licked her dry lips and looked up to the sky. Her dad had done a lot of bad, but in turn he had done a whole lot of good as well. She could only hope that he had found peace wherever he had ended up in the afterlife.

Suddenly the pain that she felt inside became so real that she had to clench her fist and back away from the window. She inhaled sharply and closed her eyes, trying to find a happy thought. She couldn't. Instead, her ears tuned in to the sound of running water and she opened her eyes up again. Without realizing what she was doing, her feet led her to the bathroom door to her right and she pushed the door open.

She stepped into the steamy bathroom and released her hair from the bun and let it drop freely around her face. Through the see-through glass of the large, rounded shower, she saw Cane standing there naked with his head toward the huge showerhead on the ceiling. The steam made it impossible for her to see his whole body; only the top half was visible. She didn't remove any of her clothing; she just wanted to feel the heat from the shower on her body.

When she opened up the shower door, Cane turned his head and was shocked to see her standing there. "Davita, what are you doing, ma?"

Day didn't say a word. She just shut the glass door behind her and went and stood directly in front of him. Her hair curled as soon as the water hit it, and she looked up at him with needy eyes. Her tears welled up but when they dropped they just blended in with the water from the showerhead. She blinked up at him and put her soft hands on his chest.

"I hurt so bad," she whispered. She swallowed her spit and breathed deeply through her mini sobs. "I keep trying to act like I'm okay, but I'm not. I am so scared and I have never been scared in my life. I feel so alone. This pain I feel, it's unbearable, and I just want it to go away. Please make it go away."

Cane looked down at her and already knew what she wanted him to do, but he couldn't. There had been many days when she would come and do collections that he would envision all of the things that he would do to her body, but he knew he couldn't. She was a conflict of interest. At that moment she had definitely caught him slipping and he wanted her to leave the bathroom the same way that she had entered it; but looking in her face he could tell that she was hurting. Never had a woman been able to pull any emotion from his cold heart, but there was something about Day that turned him soft every time. He talked his shit to her when she talked it to him, but little did she know that nobody had ever been able to speak to him the way she did without catching a bullet to the dome.

"Day, I can't," Cane said softly, placing his hands over hers and trying to gently remove them from his chest. "We can't."

"Please. I don't want to hurt badly anymore. Make me hurt good."

Day stood on her tiptoes and pressed her lips against his. He almost got lost in the softness of them and even allowed their tongues to intertwine before he jerked his neck back.

"Day. Your dad, he—"

"He's dead." Not wanting to hear him tell her no again, she dropped to her knees and took his whole nine inches of thickness in her mouth.

"Ahh!" Cane moaned over the sound of the running water. It was too late; she had already sucked the tip of his head the way that he liked it. There was no turning back. He gripped the back of her wet head and helped her bob her head back and forth. She was licking and slurping on him so good that he knew he would have been a fool to truly turn her away. He forced his dick to the back of her mouth and felt her do swallowing motions on his tip. "Dammit, Day."

He tasted so good in her mouth, and his crotch smelled like Dove body soap. She liked the way his fingers clenched and unclenched the back of her head when she flicked her tongue in a way that she liked. If she could, she would stay on her knees all day pleasing him, but he had other plans for her. He pulled himself out of her mouth and yanked her to her feet. He unzipped the drenched jogging suit outfit and ripped the cami and bra that she wore under it. Once her upper body was completely exposed he lifted her up in the air so that their lips could meet again. Wrapping her legs around his waist she ground her crotch into his hardness as she kissed and sucked on his lips. Cane used his index finger and his thumb to flick and pinch on her erect nipple while they kissed.

"Mmmm," she moaned into his mouth because the miniature pain was one that she liked. She felt her clit swell, and she knew that the moisture between her legs wasn't from the shower.

Cane put her back against the brick wall of the shower and lifted her up higher so that he would have complete access to her breasts. He massaged them as he licked and sucked, going back and forth. Her eyes were closed while she relished the feeling, and she felt the walls to her pussy squeezing and letting go. She was ready for him to be inside of her, but he wasn't ready quite yet. Standing her up gently on her feet he pulled her wet pants off and saw that she was wearing no panties. He had no complaints; he just put her clit in his mouth and sucked on it like it was a fruit.

"Cane!" she screamed and placed her hand on his wet cornrows. "Cane! Cane! Yes!"

She put a leg over his shoulder and he surprised her when he hiked her other one up too. He stood to his feet and continued to beat her clit up with his tongue while she was in the air. Her legs were shaking so badly that she was scared he would lose his grip on her and drop her, so she tried to make him put her down.

"I got you," he said, looking up at her. "Now give me this pussy. You came in here to give it to me, right?"

She bit her lip and nodded her head, allowing him to place kisses on her love box once more. It didn't take long after that for her to come all in his mouth, and she loved that he drank every drop. Once she was done shaking and screaming from her first orgasm, Cane helped her slide down his body, but he kept her legs wrapped around his waist. He kissed her on her neck and on her lips and she closed her eyes so that she could relish the feeling. She didn't even feel him walking, and when she opened her eyes again they were in his bedroom and he was laying her down on the edge of his bed. He was standing over her still wet, and the way the water was dripping down his toned body turned her on. She used her right middle finger to swirl around her still throbbing slit and she watched him watch her.

"You nasty," he said, licking his lips and lowering his eyelids at her.

"Fuck me," she whispered just loud enough to be heard.

Cane read her lips and thought about saying no. He couldn't believe that he had let it go that far. Looking down at her thick body, the image of her ass shaking while he fucked her was enough for him to push any guilty feelings out of his mind.

"You want me to fuck you?" he said, and flipped her over so that she was on her knees and her back had a perfect arch. "You want me to take your pain away? Huh? Is that what you want?"

"Yes. Ahhhh!" Day screamed when she felt his monster invade her tightness. He was so big and he didn't start off slow, so it hurt at first. She gripped his sheets and gritted her teeth until the pain subsided and the amazing pleasure came.

"Take this dick, Day," Cane coached her. "Throw it back on me. You be talking all that shit. Throw that ass back."

She had to accept the challenge because he was right; she had talked all that shit to him like he was beneath her. Now he was inside of her and she was loving every second of it. She met him stroke for stoke as he pounded her out. She was screaming his name again when she heard him spit, and before she could turn her head around she felt his thumb go inside of her butt. It heightened the intensity of the pleasure that she was feeling, and she just lay her chest and her head on the bed so that he could do his thing. She wanted him to hit it any way that he liked.

"You got the best . . ." Cane started, and threw his head back, moaning in the middle of his sentence. "You got the best pussy I've ever had! Fuck!"

He wasn't lying. Day's golden brown ass bounced whenever he dug deep inside of her, and whenever he pulled out she bit down on his bed. He felt like he was swimming inside of an ocean, and within fifteen minutes he felt himself about to explode. He gave her five more long and hard strokes before he pulled out and shot his cum all over her back. He had to stand there for a moment and collect his wits before he went to grab her a towel. When he came back she was balled up in a fetal position, and he hurried to wipe her back before she got the nut all over his black sheets.

He stood there and looked down at her, feeling like the lowest scum on the earth. The guilt came back tenfold as he stared at her naked body in his bed. He shouldn't have done it. He shouldn't have given into her lustful needs. The last thing he wanted to do was break her heart.

"I'm sorry," he said to her.

She looked up at him and couldn't help but to laugh at the somber expression on his naked body. "You," she said and sat up. She grabbed his hands and pulled herself up on shaky legs so that she could press her body on his. "Are so fucking fine." She kissed him deeply. "It was going to happen sooner or later. I used to see how you looked at me."

"Nah, ma." Cane shook his head. "I wouldn't have let it happen."

"But you just did," Day said. "So don't say sorry for something that you wanted to do. I'm not sorry."

"I'm not trying to hurt you, Day. In my life, love doesn't exist."

"Who said anything about love?" Day said and kissed him again. She liked the fact that with everything he was saying he still kissed her back. "I'm just saying I wouldn't mind having you around for a little longer. You know, for protection." She smiled up at him and winked, causing him to grin down at her.

"Yo, ma, you crazy," he said, and palmed one of her cheeks. "You done threw me all off. I'm supposed to be making you dinner."

She gave him a sneaky smile before pulling away from him to go put some clothes on. She felt like a new woman and any feeling of sadness that she had was washed away. She didn't know how long that feeling would last so she wanted to bask in it. Spending the whole day with him had given her a feeling of happiness that she hadn't felt in a week. On top of that, she had never had back-to-back orgasms the way that he had just made her experience. If he could do all of that in fifteen minutes she could only imagine what he could do in an hour. He had just made her feel better than she had in days. After he made her dinner, if she was still alive, she wanted to ride that ride again . . . and again.

Chapter 16

The best thing in his career finally happened.
The night after receiving the manila envelope,
Detective Avery's curiosity seemed to get the
best of him. Detective Avery didn't know who
had slid that piece of paper under the door of his
office, but he couldn't say that he cared, either.
He did acknowledge the fact that he owed them
a big thank-you. At first he was confused about
what he would find when he brought a team to
the address written on the piece of paper. It led
him to an empty field in the middle of a forest.
He was discouraged in the beginning because
they were out there for hours and didn't come
up with nothing.

"I think somebody was just playing a joke
on you, Detective," said one of the police officers Detective Avery had made come with him.
"There ain't nothing in this forest but raccoon
shit. Let's pack up and go home."

Detective Avery nodded his head; and just as he was about to agree and tell everyone to get their things together, his eyes fell on a clearing that he didn't remember checking.

"Over there." Detective Avery pointed his finger in the direction of the clearing. "Bring the dogs over there with me."

As soon as the dogs hit the clearing they began barking nonstop at something in the ground. One of them even started growling.

"Get the shovels, boys," he shouted back at the officers. "There's something in the ground over there!"

Detective Avery's heart pounded so hard in his chest that he was almost certain the officers around him could hear how anxious he was. When finally the hole in the ground was big enough the officers got in it and pulled out what it was that the dogs were barking at. It was wrapped in black garbage bags, and when the officer who had spoken to Detective Avery slit it open with a box cutter he instantly turned his head and covered his nose with one arm. The smell was unbearable.

"Looks like we got a body, sir," the officer said. "The bugs have been having a feast on his face, too."

"Call forensics!" Detective Avery could barely hold in his excitement. "I need an ID on this body ASAP!"

That same night, Detective Avery stayed in the lab until they got a positive ID from the victim's mother. He didn't care that she was sleeping; he needed her to come and ID her son. When she saw the body she broke down in a fit of screams and that was all Detective Avery needed to confirm what he already knew. The address on the paper had led him directly to where Antonio Lesley's body was buried. The lab also tested some of stains on his clothes along with some hairs found on his body and came back with an immediate match to Davita Mason's DNA.

"Got you now, bitch," Detective Avery said to himself and laughed evilly as he looked at the sheets of paper. "I got you now!"

"You sure you should even be here?" Cane asked, looking up at the building that Day's apartment was in. "What if somebody is up there waiting for you?"

"Don't nobody know where I live," Day assured him. "And if they do they probably aren't alive anymore. You coming up with me?"

"Nah," Cane said and stayed parked on the street. "I'ma just wait for you right here."

"Okay." She blew him a kiss and got out of the car. "I'll be right back. I just gotta grab like two things."

She slammed the door to his BMW shut and jogged to the front door of her condo. She was dressed casual in a pair of Levi jeans and a Victoria's Secret boyfriend tee. The pink Nike Roshes that Cane had talked her into buying were beyond comfortable, and she made a mental note to go back to the mall and get a couple more pairs. She used her key and opened the secured entry before going to stop at the doorman.

"Hey, Steve!" She smiled at the older man who had always been so kind to her. When he saw her he looked as if he was seeing a ghost. She raised her eyebrow at him. "What's wrong?"

"I didn't think you were coming back anytime soon," Steve said, playing with his watch. "You haven't been here for days. I'm so sorry. I didn't think you would come; that's why I let them in."

"Let who in?" Day said, backing away from his desk. "Let who in, Steve?"

His wide eyes darted around before he turned them back on her. "Run!" he yelled, startling her, but she did as he said.

She ran back out of the door before even making her way up to the condo but before she had even hit the last step she heard the police sirens. She was surrounded but still she tried to make a run for it. She had only taken a couple of steps when she felt herself being tackled from behind.

"I don't think so," she heard a familiar voice grunt; and he put a knee in her back. "Where do you think you're going, little bitch?"

"Who the fuck are you?" she asked with her face in the grass.

"You don't remember me?" the voice asked after she was cuffed. He lifted her to her feet and turned her to face him. "Your old friend Detective Avery? I'm insulted."

"Get the fuck off of me!" she yelled, and tried to jerk her arm away. "You don't have anything on me."

Her voice was so confident that he had to laugh at her. "I got you," he said, smiling and nodding his head. "That little clearing that you had Antonio's body in was a good hiding spot. But just not good enough."

The expression on Day's face dropped instantly and she felt like somebody had just ripped her heart out of her chest. "Huh . . . Huh . . ." She stumbled over her words.

"How?" Detective Avery asked, and pushed her forcefully toward the flashing lights. "An anonymous tip. Davita Mason, you are under arrest for the murder of Antonio Lesley. You have the right to remain silent. Anything you say can and will be used against you in a court of law. . . ."

His voice trailed off in Day's head. She looked and saw Cane in his car looking back at her helplessly through the car window. She shook her head at him, letting him know not to do anything stupid. Her mind was reeling because she had no idea who would snitch her out, if he was even really telling the truth about that. She hadn't told anybody except her dad where she had actually placed his body. She hung her head inside of the cop cruiser. Finally the law had caught up to the Mason name.

David Jr. sat with his elbows on the kitchen table and with his hands clasped together. He stared at his cell phone, willing it to ring; and whenever it did, if it wasn't who he wanted to talk to then he would simply ignore the call. Roland had called him a couple times and each time he did David Jr. told himself that he would call him back, but he never got around to it. His head was throbbing and he felt worse than a little kid who had just lost his puppy, because he had lost a lot more. Finally his cell phone began to vibrate around the table, and when he looked at it he saw a number that he did not recognize.

"Hello. This is a collect call from Davita Mason. To accept this call please press one. To decline this call—"

David didn't give the woman on the IVR time to say anything else before his thumb was jamming the number one on his phone.

"Hello?"

David Jr. heard his twin's voice on the other line, and he didn't think he'd ever been so happy to hear it. "Day," David Jr. said. "What the fuck did you do?"

"It doesn't matter." Her voice sounded sad. "They got me."

Earlier that day he had received a text from a number that he didn't have saved in his phone telling him that Davita had been arrested. When he tried to call he number back it had already been disconnected. He soon learned that he didn't even have to call Day's phone to confirm because her arrest was all over the news. The police had linked a body that they found in a forest to her and were charging her with first-degree murder. He had no doubt in his mind that she did it, but still the last place he wanted her was behind bars.

"We gon' get you out of there," David Jr. said, trying to sound believable. "They aren't gon' keep you in there if I can help it."

"You actually sound like you care." Day laughed a little bit.

"You're my sister, my twin. Of course I care."

There was quiet for a moment before Day spoke again. "Maybe Mom was right," she said, and shocked David Jr. "Maybe we should have just sold everything and moved on with our lives. Look at how we've been living for the last week. I don't want the rest of my life to be in hiding. We have enemies we have never even met because of the lifestyle we were born into. I don't know. I've just been in here thinking about shit these last few hours. I don't think this life is for me anymore, David Jr."

David Jr. heard her sniffle and he knew that she was crying. It hurt him to the core to hear her be vulnerable like that and, in a way, he felt that it was his fault. If only he had been the son King David always wanted, then Day wouldn't have ever felt the need to put on the big boy pants.

"We can talk about it more when you come home," David Jr. said. "Mac already contacted a lawyer for you. He's the best in the city, I heard."

"You have one minute remaining." The sound of the voice recording let them know that they didn't have much time remaining to talk.

"Yeah, okay," Day responded, and he could hear in her voice that she didn't believe him. "They have too much on me. They holding me in here with no bail. Tell Indigo to take good care of you, all right? And I'm sorry. I'm sorry for everything."

"I'm sorry too," David Jr. said, exhaling. "I—"

He wasn't able to say what he wanted to because the voice recording interrupted him and informed him that the call was over. All he heard on the other end of the phone was dead silence.

"I love you, sis," David Jr. said. He sat still for a moment trying to collect all his thoughts. All of his emotions bubbled together and, just like a bubble, they popped. He stood to his feet and used his strength and flipped the table over.

"Fuck!" he shouted out, and commenced tearing the whole kitchen apart. Throwing the chairs into the walls he left huge gapes in them. He ripped the doors to the cabinets from their hinges and launched all of the fine china onto the floor. He thought about his mother, his father, and his sister. He couldn't understand how it had all come to this. He had tried his hardest to get away from the life he was currently in, and it had just dawned on him that he would have never been able to run from it. It would have always found him. By the time the big kitchen was completely destroyed he fell to the floor, exhausted.

When Mac found him he was sitting in the middle of the mess he'd made with his head down. David Jr.'s shoulders heaved up and down with each deep breath that he took. Mac looked around his kitchen and, instead of being angry about all the money he had just lost, he knelt down beside David Jr. and patted him on the back.

"It's gon' be all right, son. It's gon' be all right."

"How do you know that?" David Jr. asked, staring at his red palms.

"Because you're still alive. And as long as you are alive then there is hope for all of us."

"That sounds like some shit from a movie. This is real life." David Jr. lifted up his head. "You know I spent all this time trying to run from who I am, and now when I look at myself in the mirror I don't even recognize myself. But when I look at pictures of my dad I see who I am supposed to be."

"Nah. You always have the option to write your own destiny."

"No, that's not what I meant. Before my dad died he sent me and Day on this mission to get some money from some niggas who owed."

"And?"

"I killed somebody," David Jr. said. "And I'm just now thinking about it. It doesn't bother me as much as I thought it would. That night in the bar when those hood niggas ran up in there and tried to kill me just because of who I was. The fact that you are protecting me just because of who I am. I used to wonder how Day could be so merciless and monstrous, but that doesn't have shit to do with it at all. It's just who we are."

"Killers?" Mac rested his elbows on his knees as he knelt.

David Jr. raised his head and shook his head, looking seriously into Mac's face. "Masons."

The doorbell sounded and Mac turned his head toward the noise. "That must be the take-out I ordered," he said, and then looked around the kitchen. "Which was a good call on my end. I'm glad you a millionaire now, little nigga. You gotta pay for all of this."

He patted David Jr. on the back one more time before getting to his feet and heading toward the front door. He looked out the window and saw no one standing there. Instinctively, he removed his gun from his waist and opened the door, wildly looking around.

"Who's there? Show yourself!" he called out into the evening breeze and, of course, nobody answered. He turned to step back in the house and felt his foot kick something. Looking down, he saw a manila envelope at his feet.

David Jr. had heard him yelling so he had come to see what all the noise was about. When he saw the expression on Mac's usually calm face he instantly knew something was wrong. He saw the envelope in Mac's hand and stepped forward to grab it. Once he had it ripped open he reached inside and pulled out a piece of paper with red ink on it. He felt himself swallow hard. The paper had three capital Ds written on it, but the first two were crossed out.

"Somebody set her up," David Jr. said out loud. "And now I'm next."

Chapter 17

Go kill him now! He's right there! Kill his friend, too!

"No!" the watcher sneered out loud, ignoring the voices. "Shut up. Just shut up and let me do this my way."

When are we going home?
I just want to go home!
I'm ready to go home!

"Shut up, all of you! Just stop talking!"

The watcher clutched their sweating forehead and waited for the voices to go away. Watching the face of the security guard had given great joy; however, the watcher wished that it was David Jr.'s. Hiding behind a bush, the watcher's eyes went to the Cadillac Seville that was parked outside of the house. The plates read DONNA, and the watcher smiled sinisterly.

"Let him have fun with his little girlfriend," the watcher said to the silenced voices. "Then we can kill him."

Chapter 18

Day lay on her back on the top of the bunk bed that she shared with another inmate named Alyssa. All the other inmates were out in the recreational center watching movies or playing cards for toilet paper. She loved when they were all gone because it gave her the chance to lie in silence.

Jail was no place for a woman like her, so she could only imagine what prison was going to be like. Her lawyer came to see her the day that she got brought in, and from what he told her things were not looking to be in her favor. He told her all of the evidence that they had against her and that there wasn't even a point to going to trial. The fact that she was David Mason's daughter would be enough for her to get a guilty verdict without even bringing the evidence into play. She knew that there were only two days left for the important meeting that David Jr. would have to go to, and she was sad that she wouldn't be there by his side because it was the same day as her court hearing.

The one thing Day didn't count on in jail was being tried by so many of the inmates. She was so used to the respect that she got when she was whipping through the streets that when she was hit by all of the hate it came as a surprise to her. Once it was known that David Mason's daughter was in jail with them, a lot of them wanted to have a go at her. Whether it was because her father had somebody in their family killed, or because they had gotten caught up behind running for him, either way they wanted a piece of her. She hadn't gotten into any fights yet because the guards had gotten specific instructions to not let anybody touch her until her court hearing on Saturday. It made her mad because it made her look weak to the other women, and they thought she was scared of them.

Little did she know a group of four women had gotten together and formulated a plan. What Day didn't realize was, although she kept to herself most times, she kept to herself in the same spot every day at the same time. She was a sitting duck and they wanted to take her head off. They paid a couple of girls in cigarettes and toilet paper to start a fake fight with each other so the guards wouldn't notice them all disappear back toward the cell block together. They crept up on Day's cell as she lay on the bed, looking up at the ceiling.

Day heard their feet before she saw them and, instead of giving them the attention they wanted, she kept her eyes on the ceiling. "Welcome to my humble abode," she said dryly. "How may I be of assistance to you?"

"You Davita Mason?" asked a tall, dark-skinned girl with braids that stopped at the nape of her neck.

"You wouldn't be here if I wasn't."

"Good! 'Cause I got a couple of bones to pick with you." She was dead serious, and for that Day had to laugh. "Somethin' funny?"

"Yeah," Day said, finally looking at the four misfits in her cell. Two of them were tall and skinny while the other two were short and stocky. All were different shades of brown and they rocked braids in ponytails. She couldn't guess their ages just by looking at their faces. It was true what they said. Jail aged you. "I don't know any of y'all."

"It don't matter," one of the short, stocky girls boomed, stepping forward and preparing to drag Day from her bed. "Because we know you. And we all knew your daddy. My baby daddy used to run for him when I was pregnant. When he got bumped up I took the wrap for him, but two days after they arrested me for what he did your daddy sent him on some bogus-ass run where he got killed. I had my baby in here and I can't even get out for a year. The state got her now."

"Sad story," Day said, not feeling any emotion.

"I heard what happened to him." The tall one spoke again and got close to the bed. "I heard whoever killed that nigga cut him up, shot him up, and even beat the shit out him with some brass knuckles. How does it feel to know that your daddy died so painfully?"

Day bit her lips together and sat up on her bed. They could say what they wanted to about her, but she wasn't going to let them talk down her father.

"Come on," the girl said, and then flashed a piece of metal in her hand. "Scary-ass bitch. The guards ain't nowhere around now to stop us from fuckin' you up. I'ma cut you for every hit my stepdaddy took from the drugs he bought from your daddy. Then I'ma stomp your head into the ground for every time he raped me when he was high."

Day looked around and saw that all of the girls in her room had weapons, while she had nothing but her fists. She turned her nose up at all of them. "You bitches still be cutting people in jail?" Her voice was so icy and lacked any hint of fear. "If you know who my daddy is and if you know my mothafuckin' name then you know how I get down." She jumped down from the top bunk and walked up to the tall girl, who looked like she was hesitating to use her shank.

"Cut her, Diamond!"

"Yeah, slice that ho!"

"Bitch, I wish the fuck you would cut me." Day tried to put as much power as she could in her voice when she got in her face. "It don't matter if I'm in jail. I got pull on the streets no matter where I reside. I'll get yo' ass rung up by ya neck in your sleep. Keep fuckin' with me."

Day stared into Diamond's eyes until she blinked. When she did, she lowered her weapon and took a step back. She had seen something in Day's eyes that she had never seen in anybody's and she knew she was probably speaking the truth. The last thing she wanted to do was wake up and see a hooded figure over her with a rope in their hand.

She shook her head at Day and stepped back. "Come on, y'all. Let's go," Diamond said and turned to leave the cell. "I ain't fuckin' with this crazy-ass bitch."

It was clear that she was the ringleader and they did whatever she said, because they followed suit without another word.

"And tell all them other bitches that shit too. Princess Davita is in this mothafucka! Don't try me!" she yelled after them before getting back on her bed and once again getting lost in her thoughts.

Indigo took the piece of paper from David Jr. and studied it. "This is some sick shit." She shook her head, seeing that two of the Ds were crossed out. "Who would do this?"

David Jr. shrugged his shoulders. "According to Mac, my dad had too many enemies to keep track of. He's installing new security equipment as we speak."

The two of them sat cuddled up on the leather couches in Mac's basement. David Jr. was beyond pissed off at the revelation that whoever was toying with them had gotten Day caught up with the feds. He knew that she would have preferred death over that any day.

"I don't know why he won't just show his face. Pussy-ass nigga." David Jr. clenched his fist.

"Whoa, chill out, big man," Indigo said. "He's not here and you're safe for now; that's all that matters. When do you think you'll be able to go home?"

"Shit, never," David Jr. said. "I'm moving out that spot as soon as this meeting is over."

"Right, I understand. You might turn on your shower and the whole place might go up into flames." David Jr.'s body went rigid at her remark and it didn't go unnoticed by her. "Oh, my. I'm sorry, David Jr. I didn't mean it like that. I just meant, you never know if he's been in your apartment. He's playing a sick game."

David Jr. relaxed his body. "Yeah, it is a sick game. I thought that these types of people just ran up in people's houses and shot guns at people."

"I guess the times are changing."

"Whatever it is, I can't wait until he comes at me," David Jr. said seriously. "Because I'm going to be ready."

"Are you now?"

"Hell, yeah," David Jr. said. "I'm not going to be caught slipping. I'm the last Mason standing."

"Mmm." Indigo licked his lips, and slid from his lap to the floor. "You know what I want to see standing?"

He smiled down at her, watching her unzip his pants and remove his bulging member. He hadn't had sex since the last time with her on the elevator, and that was the longest he'd ever gone without getting pussy.

"Hsssss," he hissed when she put her perfectly glossed lips around the head. "That feels so good, baby."

She bobbed her head up and down on him for about five minutes before she was ready to sit on it. She removed the leggings and thong that she was wearing and tossed them on the couch beside him. Climbing on top of his lap, she straddled his waist and lifted up his black Stussy shirt so her juices wouldn't stain it.

"I'm falling for you, David Jr.," she whispered and slid down on him slowly. "You make me feel so—mmmmm—good."

He gripped her by her hips and pulled her forcefully down on him with each stroke. The way her face twisted whenever the tip of his dick tapped her love box was turning him on. He put his head in her neck and began to suck it as he pumped upward at her, matching her strokes.

"I think I'm falling for you too, Indigo," he whispered in her ear; and he felt her pussy walls bite his shaft when she heard him.

"Say it again," she moaned. "Tell me you love me, David Jr."

"I love you, Indigo." He wasn't sure if he meant it, but it sounded like the right thing to say at that moment.

"I love you too, David Jr. Ohhhh, fuck me! Fuck me harder!"

"Harder?" David Jr. asked and threw her on her back. He placed her legs behind his head and put his hands behind her knees to hold them in place. He gave her powerful, quick thrusts and watched her face the twist in pure bliss. "Like this?"

"Yes! David Jr., please make me cum. I want to cum so bad, daddy!"

He gave her what she wanted because soon after he felt a warm liquid squirting on his stomach. It was too much for him. He pulled out and released all over her shaved kitty. His body jerked at the intensity of his orgasm and he breathed heavily. Sweat had formed all around his forehead and he grinned.

"Thank you," she whispered up at him. "That felt so good. I don't think I can ever get enough of you."

"You couldn't stand me when you first met me," he told her, releasing her legs.

"That was then. This is now," she told him with sincerity in her voice. "I feel like all this shit, even though it's crazy, has brought us closer together."

"Me too," David Jr. said and helped her sit up.

"Can I take a shower here?"

"Yeah, but do you have clothes?" David Jr. said and motioned to her panties and leggings on the couch. He had laid her on top of them while he was fucking her and they had just gotten all wet.

"Yes," she told him and gave him a quick kiss on the cheek. "I have some in the trunk of my car. Give me some sweatpants or something to throw on when I get out of the shower, though."

"A'ight. Let me show you to the bathroom."

Mac walked into the visitation area of the correctional center where Davita was being held. He waited patiently at the table for them to bring her out to him. He had told David Jr. that he was out getting equipment to set up security cameras around the house, and that was half true. He didn't tell him that he was going to the jailhouse, because he didn't want him to see Davita like that. He had the house completely secure and had a body on almost every inch of his house while he was gone.

When they finally brought her through the doors he forced a smile on his face, although there was nothing happy about the greeting. She returned his pained smile and embraced him before taking a seat across from him. There were a few other inmates currently visiting with their families, and Day smiled when she saw the look in the eyes of an inmate holding her baby. The little boy couldn't have been even one year old, and it saddened her to think about the pain the mother must have felt to not be able to see him grow on a day-to-day basis. She cleared her throat and turned her attention back to Mac.

"You done got yourself into some shit this time, girl," Mac started, looking across the table and into her tired face. "What the fuck were you thinking?"

"About not getting caught up behind a snitch." She thought about it and then laughed at the irony. "But now look at me. Caught up behind a snitch."

"What you talking about, Davita?"

"Detective Avery told me that he got some anonymous tip," Day said, shrugging her shoulders. "I almost didn't believe him until they showed me the pictures of Antonio's corpse."

"I thought your father taught you to always burn the bones."

"Well, I fucked up this time," Day said, and looked down at the table before the tears could fall. She decided to change the subject. "How is my brother?"

"He's coming into himself," Mac responded. He was about to tell her about the letter that was left at his doorstep, but decided against it. It was obvious that she was already dealing with enough stress. And as sad as it was, at least with her in jail he knew she was out of harm's way. "He is finally starting to accept who he is. Which will be good for the meeting on Saturday."

"Why is this meeting so important, Mac?" Day asked. "And why didn't Daddy pull me to go too?"

Mac sat up in his seat and leaned in closer so that he could lower his voice and she could still hear him. He rubbed his hands together before he spoke. "David Jr. is supposed to meet the connect in two days. After Saturday he will officially be the new king of St. Louis. King David was planning to retire, and he was going to pass the torch down to his son."

"Why couldn't he pass the torch to me?"

"Look at where you are now, Davita. You are a liability. Your head is too hot, and you have a hair-trigger temper. A kingpin never rules based off his emotions. His moves are duly calculated, and we both know that isn't you. You are meant to be beside the king. His shooter. You are trained to go. But that is besides the whole point. The point is that King David was going to let David Jr. do whatever he wanted with the empire."

"David Jr. would have wanted us to go legit."

"Exactly."

Davita got it suddenly. King David would never be able to go legit himself. He had built his whole life around the dirty money and the money laundering. He wouldn't be able to just bow out, unless he passed down his crown.

"Damn," Day said.

"Yeah," Mac told her. "That's why I gotta keep that little nigga alive for two more days."

"Please don't let nothin' happen to my brother. He at the house by himself?"

"Nah." Mac shook his head. "His lovesick ass is there with that girl. But I think it's a good thing with all the shit going on around us. I done seen a lot of shit in my days, but this? Never."

"Yeah, I . . ." Suddenly it seemed like a light bulb went off over her head. "You said he at the house with Indigo?"

Her mind was going a mile a minute. She remembered the last night she was at Mac's house and how she had gone upstairs by herself. That night was a blur, but she remembered Indigo coming up the stairs behind her. She remembered getting drunk and mentioning to her some of the things she had done in her past; but she didn't know if she had told her about what she did to Antonio.

"Do you know her last name?"

"No, why?"

"Because that night I was at your house I think I might have let too much slip to her about this whole thing," she said. "And whenever something happened she was right there. I don't know, maybe I'm tripping."

"You know, when I first saw her I thought she looked familiar, but I can't place her fa—" His eyes got big out of nowhere. "Oh, shit."

"What?"

"I have to go! I know who it is. I have to go." He stood up but Day caught his arm.

"What's going on?"

"Day, I have to go," Mac said urgently. "He's about to die."

Chapter 19

David Jr. let the water run down his body in the shower and he flexed his muscles. Indigo had showered ahead of him and he got in as soon as she got out. He'd given her a pair of his basketball shorts and a T-shirt for when she decided to go out and grab her own clothes. After he got done rinsing himself off, he got out and wrapped a white towel just below his navel. He grabbed the toothbrush that the security had gone to the store and grabbed for him so he could brush his teeth. The last thing he wanted to do was be talking all in Indigo's face with stinky breath.

He looked at himself in the mirror and took notice that he needed a touch-up on his fade. The diamonds in his ears gleamed in the light and he licked his lips, much like LL Cool J did. He put on a pair of Nike basketball sweats with the matching T-shirt and socks before he stepped out of the bathroom.

As soon as he took the first step out of the bathroom on the upper part of the house, he saw that the light in the hallway was out. He was sure that he had turned it on before he got in the shower.

"Hello?" he called out, thinking that Indigo was playing a trick on him. "Indigo?"

There was a loud shattering sound on the floor below him, followed by a spine-tingling scream.

"Indigo!" he shouted, and took off toward the stairs in the pitch-black darkness. "Indigo!"

"David! Hel . . . Ahhhhhhh!"

David didn't remember a time in his life that he ran faster than he did at that moment. The whole house was quiet and he didn't see any of the security guards. He didn't pay that any attention, however. His only focus was getting to Indigo before something happened to her. The scream had come from the dining room.

"Indigo!" David shouted, using his hands to feel on the walls for a light switch. When he found one he flipped it on, but nothing happened. The house stayed dark. "Indigo!"

"Right here," a low voice said in the dark.

He turned around, but it was too late. Something hard and heavy came crashing down on his temple, knocking him out cold.

***

When David Jr. finally came to, his chin was on his chest and his body was lurched forward slightly. His head was throbbing and he tried to open his eyes, but even the dim light that lit the room he was in pained them. Everything around him was a blur and it seemed like the room was spinning. He tried to move his arms but soon he realized that he was bound to a chair, both his arms and his legs.

Glancing around, he realized that he was in a place that he recognized. The chair that he was tied to was in the living room of his family's cabin. He hadn't been there in years but he saw hanging from the walls pictures of him and Day, and he knew that he was right. In the room beside him he could hear somebody mumbling, but he had to strain his ears so that he could make out the words. It was the strangest thing he had ever witnessed. He could tell that it was one voice speaking; however, the voice kept changing timbre, almost like there were two people in the room.

"Kill him now. Kill him now."

"No! I can't. He said he loves me."

"He will never love you! You killed his parents."

"No, he loves me. I know he does."

"Stupid bitch. You haven't even dated him for two weeks yet. How can he love you?"

"Shut up! Just shut up!"

"In . . . Indigo?" David Jr. called out. "Indigo, is that you?"

He saw her shadow first before her small frame entered the room. She was dressed in all black and in her hand she carried a big butcher knife. "David Jr., honey, you're awake!" She moved her feet quickly and bent over him to examine the gash on his head. "Damn, that looks like it hurts!"

She touched it and he jumped slightly at the sting. "Oh, I'm sorry. Does it hurt?" She giggled.

"Yo, what's going on, Indigo? If this is your idea of being kinky I'm not with it at all."

"Shut up!" she yelled in his face with a voice that he'd never heard her use before; but then she put her fingers to her lips like she'd made an accident. "Oops, sorry. I didn't mean that, David Jr., really I didn't."

"What's going on, Indigo? Why are you doing this?"

"Because I have to," Indigo said calmly, and grabbed a wooden chair so that she could sit directly in front of him. She set the knife on her lap and let her eyes travel over his face. "I must say, you and your sister highly favor your father.

You look just like he did when I tied him to the that chair in his office."

Her words played over and over in David Jr.'s head until he finally understood. "It was you. It's been you this whole time."

It dawned on him then that the only time things didn't happen were when she was around and out in the open with him and his family. Whoever had planted the car bomb had to have already been on the property; when the note was left on Mac's front door she showed up to kick it with David Jr. moments later. It all made sense and he couldn't believe that he didn't get it until just then.

"Ding, ding, ding! Do you want a cookie for finally solving the mystery?"

"But why?"

She belted out a crazed laugh and threw her head back. Her hair was disheveled and out of the ponytail that it was in earlier. The look she had in her eyes was one of a crazed woman who was out for blood and vengeance.

"But why?" She grabbed the knife, and with a swift motion she sliced his chest and he shouted out in pain.

"Tell him why, Indy."

"Shut up! I'm about to!" She stood up and paced back and forth in front of David on top of the bearskin rug. She gripped the sides of her head and mumbled words to herself. "You want to know why I did it, David Jr.? Huh? Because your father was a monster! He was like a disease that infected everybody he came into contact with."

"What did he do to you?" David Jr. panted. He looked down and saw that his white shirt was already heavily stained from the gash she had just given him.

"He ruined my life!" Indigo shouted. "He took away everything that I ever loved! Look at me! Look at me, David Jr. Who do you see?"

David Jr. tried to focus on her face but, with the blood he was losing mixed with the aching on his head, he just couldn't. She was a blur.

"I don't know, Indigo. I don't know."

"My real name is Indigo Donna Chambers. I was named after my father. Donovan Chambers."

"You're . . . you're Donovan's daughter?"

"That's what the fuck I said, isn't it?" She swung the knife again and sliced open his upper arm. He fought against his restraints and tried to eat the pain that he was feeling. "Your father had my father killed in this very same cabin. His men sent his head in a box to my mother and me. In a fucking box! When he was murdered we lost everything. We didn't have a dime to our names because your father cleared out his accounts. I got kicked out of school and my mother stopped being able to get my medication. One night I had one of my . . . episodes and she wasn't able to calm me down."

"What happened to her?"

"I killed her, duh." Indigo giggled and shrugged her shoulders like the answer was just that obvious. "She shouldn't have gotten in the way of the knife."

"You're sick," he panted.

"Hmm, maybe. Anyways, after I killed her I vowed to make all of you hurt the way you have made me hurt. My whole life fell apart the day your father killed my daddy! Over some money? Over money! Like he didn't have enough of that already! So before our date I followed him to Club Low and caught him slipping from behind, literally. I put the bomb in Day's car that day I was visiting, you know, when I had excused myself to the bathroom. It was so unfortunate that it was your mother who got blown up. I was actually going to let her live, too, sad story. Then there was Day. She was so sad that night in Mac's basement. I went upstairs to comfort her and the alcohol made her let slip where she had hidden this body. Told me that the feds were investigating her on a case and, well, you know the rest."

"Crazy bitch."

She grew stiff and looked down at him. The psychotic look never left her eyes and she swung the knife with all her might back and forth on his body and sliced him at whatever spot was open. Blood dripped from the tip of the knife and she stood there panting. She didn't like the fact that he wasn't screaming. He shouted and flinched at the pain, but he didn't scream.

"You're a tough cookie, aren't you? It's okay, though. After about twenty minutes your old man cracked too. Maybe I just need to get the brass knuckles. I'll be riiiight back."

When Mac reached his home the first thing he saw were the bodies of his security dead on the ground all around his home. After seeing that, he instantly ran inside yelling for David Jr., even though he knew he wasn't going to answer. The power in the whole house had been cut off and David Jr. was nowhere in sight. Neither was Indigo. He exited the house almost as fast as he had entered it and he jumped back in his vehicle.

He could shoot himself in the foot at how naïve he had been. He knew he had recognized her face when he had first seen her in the bar with David Jr. At the time, he couldn't put a finger on it, but after talking to Day he finally understood. The day he had followed King David's orders and killed Donovan Chambers, he took him to King David's cabin in the woods, as instructed. As they beat him to a bloody pulp Mac remembered in the back of his mind Donovan mumbling something about somebody named Indigo needing her medicine. He begged them to get her the medicine she needed but they all laughed at him. Mac just thought he was talking crazy because his brain had been shaken up. He wished he would have paid attention because he would have known who was behind all of the murders and setups a long time ago.

He thought about the things they did to Donovan, the sick, sadistic things they did to him. They tormented him for hours before cutting off his head. They even mailed it home to his family with a note so they would know why he wasn't coming home. Never in his right mind would he have guessed it would have backfired on him the way that it had. Sitting in his car, he thought back to that cabin and wished that he would have done things differently.

"The cabin," he said out loud.

He pressed on the gas and floored it, hoping that his guess was the right one. If not, then David Jr. was a dead man.

Chapter 20

David Jr. sat a picnic table by himself and watched a family of four playing at the park. He smiled at them, seeing how happy they were. The park was filled with people having fun with their families. David Jr. was the only one who was alone. Yet, he felt a strange sense of peace and belonging.

"Hello, son." A voice that he thought he would never hear again boomed from over him.

David Jr. looked up and the shock read all over his face as he stared into a face that mirrored his almost exactly. He stood there in a white suit, and white dress shoes. His smile was contagious and it was apparent that he was happy to see his son.

"Dad?" he asked, and stood to embrace his father. "But how?" Then he thought about it and his face grew stale. "I'm dead, aren't I?"

King David released his son and sat on the opposite side of the picnic table, motioning for David Jr. to sit back down.

"Am I dead?" David Jr. asked again.

"I don't know." King David tapped his fingers together. "Are you?"

"I mean, if you're here that means I'm dead, doesn't it?"

"Life is all about perception, David Jr. You could be dead, or this could all be a figment of your imagination. You make the decision."

"I don't know what I'm supposed to do, Dad. Day was more cut out for this life than I. I'm lost. You left without showing me what I'm supposed to do and who I'm supposed to be."

"You see, I believe that is where I made the mistake with you. My job was never to show you how to live your own life; it was to support you in whatever decision you made. Even if that meant you would take a different path than I did. I want you to do whatever it is you want to do in life. As long as you take care of your sister, I don't give a damn if you want to be a male stripper."

David Jr. laughed and felt the tears coming to his eyes. "There was so much that I didn't get to say to you. I'm sorry for everything and I love you, Dad. I wish that there was a way that I could make it up to you."

"I love you too, son. And you can make it up to me right now."

"How?"

"By living." King David gave his son a knowing smile. "I'll always be with you. Now isn't your time. Goodbye, David Jr."

"David Jrrrrrrr.!" A singsong voice said right before he felt cold water being dumped on his face. Immediately he was snapped back into consciousness. "Wakey wakey!"

The moment that David Jr. woke up, the pain to his body came back instantly. His jaw felt like it was broken and his right eye was swollen shut.

"Don't," David Jr. whispered when she drew her fist back to punch him again. "What do you want? I'll give you anything." The last thing he wanted to do was beg for his life, but desperate times called for desperate measures. He felt like the writer who had gotten kidnapped in the movie *Misery*. All he could think of was his sister. He didn't want to leave her in the world alone. He fought the urge to nod off again, and forced his head up straight. "Do you want money? I'll give you however much you want. You'll be able to get your medicine. You'll be able to go back to school."

Indigo looked at him and chuckled at his attempt to save his own life. "Tsk. Tsk. Tsk. Bargaining won't work with me. I won't be satisfied until you are dead too. Plus, I'll have access to all of your money once you're gone anyway." She grinned sinisterly and took the brass knuckles off of her hand and placed them on the chair that she had been sitting in. From it she grabbed the stained butcher's knife again. "I'll stop toying with you now. I'm ready to feel the pressure on this knife when I plunge it into your gut."

She put her hand on his elbow to steady him, and he was too weak to try to wobble around in the chair.

"This will only hurt a lot," she said, and yanked her elbow back to drive the knife in his stomach.

Bang! Bang!

Two shots rang out in the cabin and Indigo's body jerked. Her grip around the knife loosened and it dropped on the floor next to the chair David Jr. was tied to. She fell into him and clutched his shoulders and looked square into his eyes as hers went dim. Blood spilled from her mouth as she tried to talk.

"Da . . . David Jr., I . . ."

Bang!

That time the bullet went through her back and struck her confused heart. She died on impact without finishing her statement. David Jr. looked up and saw Mac bending over with his hands on his knees, panting. He looked at the

shape that David Jr. was in and knew that if
he had gotten there a moment later he would
have been a dead man. He rushed over to where
he was bound to the chair, and threw Indigo's
lifeless body to the side.

"Crazy-ass bitch," he said and spat down on
her. He then wrapped his arms around David Jr.,
not caring about all of the blood. "Come on. Let's
get you to the hospital."

Mac used the butcher's knife to cut David Jr.
free and he almost fell to the floor. He had lost
so much blood and was so weak that he had little
to no control over his body. Mac hoisted David
Jr. up over his back. He thought back to the day
that he almost got killed and King David had
carried him to the car in that very same manner.
He felt like he was paying homage to his best
friend by making sure his son lived.

Mac strapped David Jr. in the car and pulled
his phone out of his pocket. He made a phone
call, and let his people know that they would
need a cleanup team at the Mason family cabin,
before he got back in the car to get David Jr. to
the hospital. He hoped he wasn't bruised up too
badly because Saturday was around the corner.

"Mac," David Jr. said before he nodded off in
the passenger's seat.

"What's up, son?" Mac asked, pulling off from the site where the biggest tragedy almost had taken place.

"Don't let me fuck with no more light-skinned bitches."

Chapter 21

David Jr. was released from the hospital literally hours before his big meeting on Saturday. Mac had brought an Armani two-button suit to the hospital; and even though he had stitches under his right eye he still cleaned up very nicely. In total, David Jr. had gotten 130 stitches, and the nurses said that it was by God's good grace that he was even still alive. They wanted to keep him longer, but since his vitals were back to normal and he was walking and talking fine within twenty-four hours, they could not legally hold him there. It pained David Jr. to walk but he ate the pain, and exited the hospital fixing the diamond cufflinks on his suit. He stood there in the sun, looking and feeling like a new man. Mac had told him that he was meeting the connect that day and some very important business decisions would have to be made.

"Here, put these on," Mac said and handed him a pair of Armani sunglasses to match his suit. "You're lookin' sharp, kid. Your old man would be proud. Your car is right there. The driver will take you where you need to be."

"Wait, you aren't coming with me?"

"No," Mac said apologetically. "Your sister's court date is today. And since you can't be there, I have to go in your place."

David Jr. nodded his head, understanding. He shook Mac's hand and pulled him in for an embrace. "Thanks, Mac, for everything," he said before pulling away.

"You're like a son to me," Mac said. "I would do it all over again. I guess the next time I see you I'ma be calling you King David Jr. Or what about King David II?"

"Neither." David Jr. grinned. "King David was my dad. You can call me Prince David, though."

Mac nodded out of respect, and David Jr. threw up the peace sign and got into the awaiting Mercedes-Benz. All week he had been nervous for the meeting, but at that moment he was ready for whatever his new life was about to throw at him.

He had the pistol that Day had given him on his hip for protection, and as he rode through East St. Louis he looked at the city through the eyes of a person who had never seen it before. He was ready to bring it back and make it beautiful again, like his father had once done. He reflected on the vision that he'd had when he was in Indigo's clutches, and he smiled. He didn't know if it was real, but a part of him didn't care. He knew that his dad was somewhere watching over his son, and David Jr. wanted to make him proud.

"We're here," the driver said after almost forty minutes of driving. "You are to go to the top of the building. There will be a man with a red bowtie waiting for you. I'll wait out here."

David Jr. nodded his head and stepped out of the car. He wasn't alone. Stepping out of vehicles around him were at least ten black suits who followed him into the building. At that moment he truly embraced his title and put a little bit of swagger in his step. He was Prince David, the son of King David, and that was a title that he wasn't giving back.

When he reached the top of the stairs, sure enough, there was a man wearing a tuxedo with a red bowtie. He directed Prince David where he needed to go, but tried to stop his men from coming into the room with him.

"It's cool," Prince David said when he saw the black suits were about to get buck. "I'll be out in a minute."

"Okay, Prince."

Prince David followed the man in the tuxedo through a tall wooden door that led to a room that was empty except for a round table with only one body sitting at it. His back was turned to Prince David, and when Red Bowtie shut the door he walked slowly to the table. He sat down at the chair that was directly across from him.

"So what do they call you these days?" the deep baritone voice asked. "King David II?"

"That's funny." Prince David chuckled. "You're the second person to ask me that today. But, nah, they call me Prince David. Or they will, depending on how this meeting goes."

"Oh, they will," the man said and spun his chair around. "Trust me."

When Prince David saw who sitting in the chair before him he couldn't believe his eyes. "You? You're the connect?"

"In the flesh. Now, let's talk business."

Epilogue

Day walked through the doors of the county jail and prayed that it would be her first and last time ever being there. It was a little past five in the evening and she had just gotten released. She was too tired to leap for joy, but she would be lying if she said it didn't feel good to view the world as a free woman again. She wouldn't miss anything about it. Not the food, not the clothes, and definitely not the hating-ass bitches.

She waited outside of the building wearing the same Juicy outfit that she had on when she got there, and she could not wait to get home to take a shower. Her cellmate, Alyssa, had done two neat Cherokee braids in her hair earlier that day so that she could be presentable in front of the judge.

She was happy that Mac ended up coming to her court hearing with the lawyer. Detective Avery was in the gallery and she could tell by the smug look on his face that he was convinced that he had finally brought down a Mason. She found it sad that that was something he lived for. She kept her face forward and tried to avoid eye contact with anybody.

Before they asked her how she pled, the bailiff, who of course was on Mac's payroll, slid the judge an envelope. Inside of the envelope were pictures of the judge doing many unheard-of sexual acts with teenage boys. If news of that were ever to leak, his whole career would be over, not to mention his marriage.

Day already knew what was about to happen when she saw his face turn red behind the bench, and she was grinning at Detective Avery before he dismissed all of the charges. She made sure to give the detective a wink and blow him a kiss as the guards led her away to be discharged. She could still hear his angry scream in the back of her mind.

"Where is this nigga at?" she asked herself. She had left her cell phone in Cane's car the day she had gotten arrested, so she had no way of getting in contact with her ride. She was about to say fuck it and start walking when she saw her brother's Mercedes-Benz pull up. He parked and got out of the car. Her eyes instantly went to his bruised-up face.

"Mac told me what happened," she said when he walked up to her. "You good. I also heard you calling yourself Prince David now."

"That's what you heard?"

"Yeah."

"Then I guess that makes you Princess Day." He smiled at his twin sister and she smiled back.

"That means the meeting went well then?" she asked, and his smile got even bigger while he nodded. She hesitated before she asked her next question. "So we're legit then? No more dirty money?"

Prince David looked at her and saw in her eyes that she wasn't quite ready to leave the life of a hustler behind her. And him? He wasn't ready to give it up before he had given it a chance.

"Nah." Prince David shrugged his shoulders casually. "Same ol', same ol'. Just better."

She laughed and threw her arms around her brother's neck. "I love you, brother," she said, holding on to him tightly like she would never see him again.

He squeezed her back. "I love you too, Day. We all we got now."

"Always and forever," she said and pulled away. The two walked side by side to the car. "Who is the connect, anyways?"

Prince David grinned and nodded to the car.

"He rode with me. We got some business to handle right after this. You riding?"

"He's in the car with you, David Jr.? And you came to pick me up from jail!" Day stopped in her tracks.

"Chill, ma," a voice said when the door opened. "You know I like seeing you at your best or worst."

Cane stood up from the car and looked at Day like she was the most beautiful woman on the planet. Her eyes almost bulged out of her head.

"Wait, wait, wait!" Day put her hands in the air. "First, we find out that the psycho crazy killer was David Jr.'s bitch; and now we find out that you're the connect? But you worked for my dad? Plus, you're so young!"

"Correction: I worked with your father." Cane walked to her door and opened it for her. "And your pop's original connect was my old man. He died a couple years back of colon cancer. So, just like Prince David here, the torch got passed down to me."

"Mmm, I'm fuckin' with the plug." Day winked at him and kissed him on his cheek. "I can get used to this."

Cane shut the door for her and he and Prince David got in too.

"Where are we going?"

"To the crib." Prince David made a face at her. "So you can change because you smell like old bitches."

Everybody in the car laughed. Day sat back and watched the two men mingle. She couldn't remember a time that she had felt so happy. She knew that there would be times when she would be sad, but at that moment none of that mattered. She stared at her brother and noticed something different about him. His whole aura was different and he reminded her of somebody she knew very well. He caught her gaze in the rearview mirror and she nodded at him, giving him her approval before she turned her head and looked at the sky above her. It was a clear blue sky and she knew that everything had happened the way that it was supposed to, to put the final pieces of the puzzle together.

"Thank you, Daddy," Day whispered and let a tear slide down the side of her face. "Long live King David. Forever."